THE GUNSMITH

173

JERSEY LILY

J. R. ROBERTS

JOVE BOOKS, NEW YORK

JERSEY LILY

A Jove Book / published by arrangement with
the author

PRINTING HISTORY
Jove edition / May 1996

The Putnam Berkley World Wide Web site address is
http://www.berkley.com

ISBN: 0-515-11862-1

A JOVE BOOK®
Jove Books are published by The Berkley Publishing Group,
200 Madison Avenue, New York, New York 10016.
JOVE and the "J" design are trademarks
belonging to Jove Publications, Inc.

PRINTED IN THE UNITED STATES OF AMERICA

10 9 8 7 6 5 4 3 2 1

THE GUNSMITH

173

JERSEY LILY

ONE

When Clint Adams first met Lillie Langtry he was no less enthralled by her than were all of her admirers. Lillie was a statuesque five-foot-eight, with long red-gold hair that tumbled in great waves to her shoulders when she was not wearing it piled high on her head. Her skin was pale and flawless, her face exquisite.

He saw her onstage in New York, and he knew her history. Born in England, she was rumored to have had love affairs with dukes, princes, and kings. He had no reason to believe he would ever be anything but one of her admirers. Little did he know that a friend of his, prominent in the theater, went backstage and told her that the "legendary American gunman, the Gunsmith," was in the audience. She asked that Clint be brought backstage to meet her.

In the privacy of her dressing room they met and talked. He told her how he'd enjoyed her performance, and she told him she wanted to hear all about his "notoriety." He informed her politely that he never discussed that.

"Not even with me?" she asked coquettishly.

"Reputations are not all they're made out to be, Miss Langtry," he said. "It's really not very interesting at all."

They were seated on a plush sofa she had insisted on having in her dressing room. She was still dressed for the stage, with a low-cut gown that revealed a most enticing cleavage. In fact, he was caught between looking at her lovely face and her equally lovely breasts.

"I rather doubt that, Mr. Adams . . . and please, call me Lillie."

"And you must call me Clint."

"Very well, Clint. Would you do me the pleasure of dining with me this evening?"

He was clearly surprised by the invitation.

"Why are you so surprised by my invitation?" she asked.

"Well, your reputation indicates that you, uh, prefer more . . . royal company. Kings and princes and such."

"I prefer the company of interesting men," she said. "Are you an interesting man, sir?"

"I hope that I am," he said.

"Very well, then," she said, leaning forward so that he had no choice but to look at her cleavage, "why don't we let me be the judge of that?"

"All right," he said, "dinner it is."

"I have to change and get ready," she said. "Would you return for me in one hour?"

"It would be my pleasure, Miss—Lillie."

They stood up and she presented her hand. Conscious of where she came from, where men routinely kissed the hands of ladies, he nevertheless simply took it and held it for a brief moment. She seemed to like that.

"I think it will be an interesting evening," she said as he walked to the door, "for both of us."

And it was.

When he had entered the theater for her performance, he had never expected to get the chance to meet Lillie Langtry. He was even more surprised, then, when later that night he found himself in bed with her.

He returned within the hour and she was ready. She was wearing another low-cut gown, and her hair was piled high atop her head. She had a beautiful, graceful neck, and Clint found himself wondering what it would feel like beneath his lips.

There were other men waiting outside the theater for her, calling out offers only men of great wealth could offer, but she paid them no mind as she and Clint walked to a waiting buggy.

"Where shall we go?" she asked. "Have you been to New York before?"

"Once or twice," he said.

"Then you choose the place."

"Very well," he said, and called out a destination to the driver.

In point of fact Clint had only been to this restau-

rant a few days earlier, taken there by the same
friend who had arranged for the introduction. It
would cost him a fortune to take Lillie there, but it
would be worth it.

As they entered she was immediately recognized.
Everyone in the place stood up and applauded, and
she reacted with grace and poise, acknowledging
them with a beautiful smile and a nod of her head.
Clint found himself relishing the feeling of going totally unrecognized.

They were shown to a table by a very appreciative
waiter, who returned moments later with a bottle of
champagne, "compliments of the house."

"I am amazed by your poise," Clint said candidly.
"It's not usually found in one so young."

She laughed and said, "You think I am young?"

"I do."

"You're either a marvelous liar, Clint Adams," she
said, "or a delightful man."

"Perhaps," he said, pouring the champagne, "a little of both."

TWO

Dinner was fascinating for him, as she talked of the many places she had been and the many lovers she'd had. As he listened he was aware that she was not so much bragging as she was simply telling him a lot of the interesting things that had happened to her.

She told him that her men were mostly weak and easily dominated. She cited the Prince of Wales, Crown Prince Rudolph of Austria-Hungary, American millionaire Fred Gebhard. And her husband, Edward Langtry, was, she said, "A sexual dud.

"George Baird," she went on, "delighted in beating me, but I made him pay five thousand pounds for the privilege."

She regarded him across the table with an amused look on her face.

"You are not intimidated," she said.

"Oh, but I am," he said, "but by your beauty, not by your stories."

"Most men," she observed, "would be intimidated by both."

"I'm not most men."

"I'm beginning to realize that," she said, "but I've talked enough about myself—even though it is my favorite subject. I want to hear about you, about the famous Gunsmith."

"Tell the truth," he said. "You never heard of me until Gerald Wilson told you I was in the theater."

"That's true," she said sheepishly, "but he told me of your legend—"

"Gerald has a big mouth."

"But if he hadn't told me of your legend," she said, "then I would not have discovered what a delightful man you are."

"I suppose that's true."

She leaned forward and put her hand on his. He was aware that they were the object of the attention of every other person in the room. He was also aware of the heady scent rising from between her breasts. He enjoyed all of it.

"If you do not want to talk about it, you don't have to," she said.

"Thank you."

"We shall just eat," she said haughtily, "and talk of nothing."

"Well," he said, "I could talk a *little* about myself. . . ."

He told her how he had come to the West from the East at a young age, how he had become involved with guns, discovering that he could not only take them apart and put them back together, but that he had a natural ability to shoot them.

"You mean you were simply able to hit what you aimed at with a pistol?"

"I don't even have to aim," he said. "I simply point the thing, as if it was an extension of my finger."

"And you can hit anything?"

"Anything."

"No matter the size?"

"Anything."

"No matter if the object is moving or standing still?" she asked.

"Anything."

She smiled.

"What?" he asked.

"You are bragging."

"No brag," he said, "just fact."

"Prove it."

"Here?"

"No," she said, "not here. Tomorrow, someplace where you can prove it."

He thought it over for a moment, and then decided, Why not?

"All right," he said. "Tomorrow."

THREE

When the cab pulled up in front of Lillie's Park
Avenue hotel she looked at Clint and said, "Well,
aren't you coming up?"

"Oh, well . . ."

She laughed, a full, rich sound that came from
deep in her throat.

"You're not worried about my reputation, are you,
Clint?"

"I guess not," he said, "not if you aren't."

"We both know what reputations are worth, don't
we?" she asked. She took his hand and said, "Come
with me."

She led him to her suite where, as soon as they
were inside, she turned and moved into his arms. She
was a solid woman and felt wonderful pressed
against him. Her mouth was avid and eager for his,

and they kissed deeply for a long time before moving apart so they could undress.

Her body was glorious, full and firm, and this was when he thought back to when he first entered the theater. He never would have expected to be here just hours later, but he was very happy that he was. He couldn't help but think that he was in a place where kings and princes had been before him.

They stood next to the bed together, and before they fell onto it, locked in a passionate embrace, he took the pins from her hair, allowing it to tumble to her shoulders. Over the next few hours he discovered Lillie Langtry to be an inventive and expert lover, but he was pleased that he was able to keep up with her very well . . . as was she.

Later, he would remember every moment he spent with her in bed. . . .

She was astride him, his penis buried deep inside of her, and she was simply moving on him, not riding him up and down, but just moving her hips side to side or rotating them. He couldn't take his eyes off her breasts. He reached for them, stroked her hard nipples, her smooth skin, then lifted his head and brought them to his mouth. He sucked first one, then the other, then squeezed them together and sucked both nipples at the same time. Her breasts were large and firm, with smooth, heavy undersides he loved to feel in his palms.

He could have spent all night concentrating on her breasts, but there were other parts of Lillie Langtry that deserved the same amount of attention. . . .

At one point he laid her down on her belly and began to touch her. He stroked her back with his fingertips, using a feather-light touch, working his way down to her buttocks, running one finger along that deep crease until his hand was between her thighs and he was stroking her. She moaned and moved her hips, but when she tried to roll over he stopped her.

"Not yet."

"You're killing me," she said.

He smiled and repeated, "Not yet."

He continued to touch her, moving his hands down her thighs and calves, until he was down by her feet. When he kissed her foot she shuddered, and when he sucked on one of her big toes she moaned and buried her face in the pillow.

He used his mouth to work his way back up now, over her calf, pausing behind her knee to use his tongue, then kissing her thighs. He spread her legs wide so he could lie down between them. He kissed her firm buttocks and used his tongue to gently probe her, teasing her until she could take no more. This time when she wanted to roll over he still would not let her, but he told her she could get to her knees, if she wanted. She did, and he knelt behind her and drove himself into her that way. She was wet and ready, and began to rock back against him in time with his thrusts. He held her by the hips and closed his eyes. Each thrust brought a new thrill for both of them, and he hoped that he could last because he wanted it to go on forever.

"Wait, wait," she said suddenly. She reached behind her and pushed him away. His penis slid free of her, wet and pulsing.

She touched her own buttocks, spread them, and said, "Here, I want it here. . . ."

He did not hesitate. He was slick enough from her that when he probed with the head of his penis he entered her more easily than he would have thought. He took his time, though, moving more and more deeply inside of her until she sighed and said, "Yes," and they started moving together again. . . .

"You are certainly not a sexual dud," she said later, breathlessly.

"Why, thank you very much," he said. "You're very good yourself."

She stretched, putting her hands behind her head and pointing her toes. He greatly enjoyed what the stretch did to the parts of her between those two points.

"I feel glorious," she said, smiling at him. She reached out and put her hand on him, rubbing him. "Where on earth did you learn to please a woman?"

"Over the years," he said. "It comes with practice."

"Well, I daresay you've had a lot of practice and have now reached the rank of expert."

"Funny," he said, "I was thinking the same about you."

"Oh, yes," she said, "I have had practice, but over the years I have encountered very few men like you—if any."

"I'm sure you've had many great lovers," he said, "if only because you brought them up to your level."

"I wish that were true," she said. "Perhaps I've

been going about this the wrong way."

"How do you mean?"

"Well, maybe I should forget about men with titles and with money. They don't seem to feel they need to try all that hard."

"Then maybe you should give us commoners more of a chance to impress you."

"Very well," she said, "I will."

She slithered down between his legs and began to touch him.

"Uh, I didn't mean now," he said, since they had just finished making love for hours.

"No, no," she said, "if you want to impress me you'll have to start now."

"I thought I just finished—"

He stopped short when she took his penis into her mouth and slid her hand beneath his testicles. She touched a spot down there that made him jump, and then she began to stroke it.

"Mmmm," she said appreciatively as he started to swell, surprising even himself.

He became fully hard in her mouth, and she began to suck him ardently, her finger still stroking beneath his testicles. He lifted his butt off the bed as she continued to suck him, and suddenly she slid both hands beneath him, cupping his buttocks, and began to suck him harder, moving her head faster and faster until he shouted out loud and exploded into her mouth.

"Mmmm," she said, kissing her way up his thigh and over his belly, finally licking his nipples. "All right, Mr. Adams. I am sufficiently impressed."

He was out of breath, or he might have agreed with her.

Across the street from the hotel a man stood in a darkened doorway. He knew that the glorious Lillie was in her hotel room with the man she had had dinner with. He was waiting there to see what time the man would come out.

At the same time he thought of Lillie Langtry as beautiful and as a bitch, glorious and yet evil. He loved her, and he hated her.

He had watched Lillie onstage at every one of her performances all week long, and he had followed her each time afterward. Many men had courted her during her stay in New York, and taken her to dinner, but this was the first man she had taken up to her room with her.

The slut.

He didn't know why this man had been so fortunate, but he knew one thing—he would not be so fortunate when he came out.

FOUR

Clint left Lillie lying on her stomach, drifting off to sleep. She had to be at least as pleasantly fatigued as he was. He was the one who decided that he would go back to his own hotel and pick her up later that day for a picnic in Central Park. He had chosen the park as the place where he would demonstrate for her his abilities with a gun. She had informed him that she was holding him to his promise to do that. . . .

"I don't remember promising," he said.

"I remember it very well," she said, sliding her hand down between his legs and taking hold of him.

"Okay, okay," he said quickly, "I remember my promise."

"And you will keep it?"

14

"Yes."

"Tomorrow?"

"Yes."

She released her hold on him and said, "I knew you were a man of your word."

He dressed as quietly as he could and left the room without waking her. Walking down the hall he once again had to shake his head at his good fortune. All he'd thought he would be doing that night was going to the theater to watch her perform. What had happened after that had been beyond his wildest imaginings.

He walked down the winding staircase to the lobby, wondering if anyone would recognize him as having entered the hotel with Lillie. Probably not. He already knew that all eyes were on Lillie Langtry wherever she went, it didn't matter if it was men or women. That suited him just fine. Although his notoriety did not get him as instantly recognized as hers did, he'd had plenty of experience with being recognized.

He preferred *not* being recognized.

The man across the street immediately recognized Clint as the man who had gone to Lillie Langtry's room. He watched as Clint walked out of the hotel, looked left and right—probably looking for a cab—then shrugged and started to walk.

He gave Clint a bit of a head start, then stepped out of his doorway and followed him, staying on his side of the street.

He wasn't sure yet how he was going to punish

this man, but he wanted to keep him in sight until he decided.

Clint knew that his Fifth Avenue hotel was just several blocks from Lillie's, so when he didn't see a cab immediately he decided to walk it. He was totally preoccupied with the memory of being in bed with Lillie. Her taste and smell were still with him, and her touch was right there in his mind. He was sorry that his plans called for him to leave New York the day after tomorrow, while her plans called for her to continue to perform through the next week, fulfilling her two-week commitment. He toyed with the idea of changing his plans and staying, but it was much too early for that. It remained to be seen if she would still be interested in him after tonight, or tomorrow. After all, she was notorious in Europe for leaving her lovers rather abruptly.

He turned the corner of Fifty-third Street and recognized where he was. He was only a block away from his hotel when he heard the rapid footsteps behind him. He might have heard them earlier if he had not been thinking about Lillie. He turned quickly and saw the man bearing down on him. In the moonlight he could see only gleaming teeth, the whites of the man's eyes, and the reflection of the moonlight off the blade of his knife.

He had time to lift his left arm, while with his right he grabbed for the Colt New Line that was tucked into his belt at the small of his back.

The man struck, the knife biting into Clint's left arm. The impact threw Clint off balance, causing him to stagger back. He slammed into the wall of the nearest building and was not able to get the New Line out of his belt.

As he regained his balance he looked around but could see nothing. He could hear the man's footsteps, though, as he ran away. There had been no attempt to steal his wallet. The man simply seemed intent on doing him harm, and running away.

Clint looked at his left arm. The sleeve was cut, and there was blood seeping out. It was starting to sting now, and he knew that he was going to need medical attention. He took out his handkerchief, wrapped it around the wound, and continued on to the hotel, where he hoped to catch a cab that would take him to a hospital.

He was still shaking his head at the suddenness of the seemingly senseless attack.

FIVE

The doorman at the hotel was able to get Clint a cab to take him to a hospital on Seventh Avenue. A doctor looked at the wound on his arm and pronounced it clean. He stitched it closed, then bandaged it tightly. Clint had had stitches only one time before in his life. He didn't like them, especially since they had to be administered with a needle. He wondered when doctors and seamstresses had become on the same level.

When he returned to the hotel he found a policeman waiting for him in the lobby. Clint knew one or two policemen in the city, but this was not one of them. This man introduced himself as Sergeant Delaney. He was in his early thirties, about five eight, and barrel-chested.

"I understand you had some trouble on the street, sir," the sergeant said.

"Who did you hear that from, Sergeant?"

"The management here at the hotel, sir," Sergeant Delaney said. "They take very good care of their guests."

"I guess they do."

"You were . . . attacked?"

"Yes, I was."

It took Clint only a few moments to tell the policeman what had happened.

"That is all the description you're able to give me?" the policeman asked.

"That's all I saw, Sergeant."

"Well," the sergeant said, putting away his pencil and notebook, "it could be anyone. We will check with some of the street gangs first. I suggest you get some rest."

"That was my intention, Sergeant. Uh, thanks for your help."

"I'll be in touch if we find out anything. It's too bad he didn't get your wallet."

"Why is that, Sergeant?"

"He'd be easier to identify if he had it on him when we caught him."

"Yes," Clint said, "I guess that would make him easier to identify. I'm sorry I didn't give it to him."

"Well, no matter," the sergeant said. "We'll find him sooner or later."

"I have all the confidence in the world that you will," Clint said.

He shook the sergeant's hand and watched as the

man left the hotel, then he went to the front desk.

"Who called for the police?" he asked the clerk.

"The manager, sir."

"And who told the manager what happened?"

"I did, sir," the clerk said. He was in his early twenties and eager to please. "Did I do something wrong?"

"No, that's okay," Clint said. "You did just fine."

Two days to go and he had almost managed to avoid the police completely.

That would have been a record for one of his stays in New York.

SIX

The next day Clint showed up at Lillie's hotel with a cab and a picnic basket he'd gotten from his hotel dining room. During the course of the week, having breakfast every day in his hotel, he had gotten to know one of the waiters, who was only too happy to put a basket together, especially when he found out who it was for.

"Lillie Langtry?" he asked. "The beautiful lady from England?"

"That's her," Clint said.

The waiter's name was Rocky. He was a balding man in his early forties who stood about five foot five and was very good at his job.

"Did you die and go to heaven?" Rocky asked.

"Just about," Clint said.

"How did this happen?"

Clint shrugged.

"I just lead a charmed life I guess, Rocky."

"No guessing about it, Mr. Adams," Rocky said, "you do. You wait here and I'll go and have one of the cooks put something together for you."

Clint remained at his table, drinking more coffee and waiting. When Rocky reappeared he had a huge wicker basket on one arm.

"Here ya go, Mr. Adams," he said, putting it on the table. "I hope you and Miss Langtry will enjoy it."

Clint shook his head and wondered why the waiter would even take him at his word that he was going on a picnic with Lillie Langtry.

"I heard what happened last night, Mr. Adams," Rocky said, before Clint left the dining room. "I notice you're favorin' your left arm."

"Am I?" Clint thought he'd been covering it pretty well.

"Just a little," Rocky said. "I'm just observant, ya know?"

"I'm starting to realize that, Rocky."

"Did ya talk to the police?"

"Yes, a sergeant named Delaney."

Rocky nodded.

"Conscientious," he said, "that's the word for Delaney. I don't know how good you could really say he is, but he tries, ya know?"

"I guess."

"Any ideas about who it was attacked ya?"

"No," Clint said. "I'm lucky I'm not dead. I was really daydreaming."

"Well, I can understand that," Rocky said, "considerin' where you just was—but I can't understand it considerin' who you are, ya know?"

"Believe me, I know, Rocky," Clint said. "I guess I must be getting old."

"Well, watch your step from now on," Rocky said, "or ya won't be gettin' much older, ya know?"

"I know, Rocky," Clint said, "I know."

He went out front, carrying the basket in his left hand so as to keep his right hand free. Overnight he had decided that the attack on the street had not been directed specifically at him, but that he'd simply been in the wrong place at the wrong time. For that reason he was still content to carry the Colt New Line against the small of his back.

He'd carried his gun belt down to the dining room, and before leaving discovered that there was room in the picnic basket for it. That was better than carrying it out in the open.

The doorman—a different one from the one who'd helped him last night—got him a cab and handed the picnic basket in to him. At the other end the doorman of Lillie's hotel helped him out of the cab with the basket.

"You could carry that easier if you hung it on your arm, sir," the doorman said.

"I know," Clint said. "Thanks. Would you hold this cab here, please?"

"Yes, sir."

He couldn't hang the basket on his left arm because of his bandage, and he didn't want to compromise his gun hand—just in case.

He went inside and had the desk clerk send a bellboy up to Lillie's room to tell her he was there. When she came down the circular staircase she stopped all activity in the lobby.

"You look lovely," he said as she reached him. He saw that she had remembered to bring a blanket.

"Thank you," she said. "I slept well. Did you?"

"Yes."

"Shall we go?"

He led her out to the cab, where the doorman helped them get in.

"What's wrong with your arm?" she asked when they were seated.

"Oh, it's nothing."

"You're favoring it," she said. "It is most certainly something."

"All right," he said, and as the cab started to move he told her what had happened last night while he was walking back to his hotel.

"That's horrible," she said. "Are you sure you're all right?"

"Yes, I'm fine."

"Did you know the man?"

"I never saw him before," Clint said. Then he added, "Well, I really can't say that with any certainty, because I didn't get a good look at him."

"Why not?"

"Because I was thinking about you," he said, and then knew he shouldn't have said it.

"You mean you almost got killed because of me?" she asked, aghast.

"Not really, Lillie," he said. "I almost got killed because of my own carelessness. I let my guard down, which is something I never do."

"And you did it because of me."

"No, not because of you. Maybe after all these years I'm just getting careless."

"Maybe," she said, putting her hand on his leg, "you should have stayed with me last night."

He smiled and said, "I think you're right."

"Was it a robbery?"

The man had made no move to grab Clint's wallet, but he decided to let Lillie believe that's what it was.

"I'm sure that was it," Clint said, "an attempted robbery."

"Have you talked to the police?"

"I have. I'm sure they'll catch the man. Let's not talk about him the rest of the day, okay?"

"Very well," she said. "Did you bring it?"

"Bring what?"

"Don't tease me, Clint," she said. "Did you bring your gun?"

"Oh, that. Yes, it's in the basket."

"Excellent," she said. "This is so exciting. How many targets will you shoot for me?"

"As many as I can," he said, "before the police come and stop me from firing my gun in the park."

SEVEN

The cab took them right into Central Park at Fifty-ninth Street, where Clint had been only once or twice, and not on happy occasions. Someone had once tried to kill him in the park. He hoped that wouldn't happen this time.

They spotted a likely place for a picnic and told the driver to stop. The man jumped down from his seat to help Lillie down from the cab, and she charmed him with one smile. She was wearing a high-necked dress today, and her red hair was piled atop her head and beneath a broad-brimmed hat.

"Thank you," she said, and the man blushed.

Clint paid him and sent him on his way.

"It's amazing," he said, taking her hand. She carried the basket, because of his arm. He carried the blanket.

"What is?" she asked.

"The effect you have on men," he said. "You seem to be able to turn them all into bashful little boys."

"Men *are* little boys," she said. Then she amended her statement and added, "Most men, that is."

They found a grassy knoll and he spread the blanket. They sat on it and she removed her hat, patting her beautiful hair to make sure it was in place.

"What do we have for lunch?" she asked.

"I don't really know," he said. "The cook at my hotel packed it for me."

"Then we'll both be surprised."

They *were* surprised, and pleasantly so. They found cold chicken, as well as sandwiches, hard-boiled eggs, and two bottles of champagne.

"Your cook was very thorough," she said. "We will have to finish both bottles of champagne."

"And why is that?" he asked.

She held one up and said, "So you can shoot them."

He laughed and said, "If we drink two bottles of champagne I won't be able to hit anything."

"And that would be disappointing," she said. "Very well, I will make the supreme sacrifice."

"No champagne?" he asked.

"No, silly," she said, "I'll just have to drink most of it myself."

They feasted on lunch and left very little for the ants. With lunch they managed to finish one bottle of champagne, and as promised Lillie drank most it. She seemed to have an amazing constitution, for the champagne seemed to affect her very little, if at all.

"All right," she said, "it's time. Have you ever done this kind of shooting before?"

"I've competed in contests before," he said.

"What kind?"

"Sharpshooting, trick shooting, all kinds."

"Did you win?"

"Usually. One time Buffalo Bill Cody himself offered me a job with his show."

She clapped her hands together and said, "I met him in France, when he was doing his show there. What a fascinating man."

"Really?" Clint asked. "Did you, uh . . ."

"Oh, no," she said, "Colonel Cody was a perfect gentleman. He had a young lady with him, though, who was wonderful with a gun."

"Annie Oakley."

"That was her. Can you outshoot her? Did you?"

"We never competed," he said.

"Could you outshoot her, though?"

"I wouldn't like to say," he answered.

"Why not?"

"There are different kinds of shooting," Clint said. "Annie is wonderful with a rifle. She can shoot the heart out of an ace at almost any distance."

"Can you do that?"

"With a handgun," he said, "but Annie uses a rifle most of the time."

She cocked her head and looked at him.

"I think you just don't want to admit that a woman might be able to outshoot you."

He laughed and said, "Well, if any woman could, it would be Annie."

Now she looked at him with renewed respect.

"Even that is quite an admission," she said. "You constantly surprise me, Clint Adams."

"Well, I think that's good, don't you?"

"Oh, yes," she said, "it's very good."

EIGHT

"What shall we shoot at first?" Lillie asked.

"We?"

"Well," she said sweetly, "you are going to teach me how to shoot, aren't you?"

"We never said anything about teaching you how to shoot," Clint said.

"Don't you think I can learn to shoot?"

"Anyone can learn to shoot, Lillie."

"Do you think I could learn to shoot as well as Annie Oakley?"

"I doubt it," he said. "Not unless you started out with an eye for it."

"Well," she said triumphantly, "how will we know that unless I start?"

"Haven't you ever fired a gun before?"

"I have never had occasion to do so," she said.

"Men usually defend my honor, so I have not yet had the need to fire a weapon."

"If I'm any judge," he said, "I think you can depend on men defending your honor for a very long time."

"Oh, nonsense," she said. "Who will defend my honor when I'm a shriveled up old lady of eighty?"

"A shriveled up old man of eighty?" he offered.

"Very well," she said, "if you don't want to teach me then at least shoot at something."

"Shoot at what?" he asked. Then he added, "And remember, we may be stopped at any time by a policeman. This is, after all, a public park."

"It's a huge park," she said. "We could probably shoot for hours before they find us."

"All right, then," he said, "pick a target."

"Let's start with this," she said, indicating the empty champagne bottle.

"Where would you like to put it?"

She stood up and began to look around.

"Wait," she said, and then ran about twenty yards away before turning. By the time she did, he had his holster strapped on.

"Could you hit it here?"

"Yes."

She moved another ten yards.

"Here?"

"Yes."

Another twenty.

"Certainly not here?" she called out.

He was tempted to shoot the bottle from her hand, teaching her a lesson, but he decided not to.

"Just put it down and stand away," he said.

She set it on the ground and then moved away about five feet.

"Move further away from it," he called out.

"Why? Are you afraid you'll hit me?"

"You might be hit by flying glass."

She smirked and said, "Then just shoot off the top of it."

Before she could enjoy her smug remark he pointed and fired. The top of the bottle flew off, the rest remained standing.

Lillie stood staring at it, then looked at him and frowned.

"I'm going to move it further away."

"Not too far," he said. "I don't have a rifle."

She picked up the bottle, turned and looked around, then turned back.

"Can you hit it if I toss it in the air?"

"Yes."

"All right, then," she said, "let's do that."

He decided to be a bit smug himself.

"Do you want me to hit it on the way up," he called out, "or down?"

"You think you're so smart," she called back, "hit it both."

That meant he'd have to shoot off the rest of the neck on the way up, and then shatter the bottle on the way down.

"All right," he said, "toss it away from you, not straight up, and then move back."

She was a big, strong woman, and when she tossed the bottle into the air it was not an easy toss. The bottle rose with velocity, tumbling end over end. He had to wait until the tumbling slowed, but the bottle was still ascending. He fired one shot, and the neck of the bottle snapped off.

His shot changed the trajectory of the bottle. Instead of continuing up, it jumped to the right, and then started down. He fired, and his bullet shattered it while it was still about ten feet in the air.

He turned and executed a small bow, and Lillie began to walk toward him, applauding.

"Satisfied?" he asked.

"Almost," she said.

"Why almost?"

"I have one more thing I would like you to shoot at," she said.

"What's that?"

She bent over and picked something up, then showed it to him.

It was the cork from the champagne bottle.

"This!" she said triumphantly.

"Do you want to hold it while I shoot it?" he asked.

"Good Lord, no," she said, then regarded him suspiciously. "I once saw Annie Oakley shoot a cigarette from a man's mouth. You could shoot this cork from my hand?"

"I could try," he said, "but it might cost you a finger or two."

"You'd miss?"

"No," he said, "you would flinch, causing the bullet to hit a finger."

She studied him for a moment, then shook her head and said, "I'll throw it in the air."

He holstered the gun and said, "Go ahead and throw it."

"First we must wager."

"Why?"

"To make it interesting."

Now he studied her suspiciously.

"You're not going to toss it very high, are you?" he asked.

"I will toss it as high as you like," she said, "but I want to wager something, just to increase the enjoyment."

"What do you want to bet?"

"If you miss," she said, "you will teach me how to shoot."

"And if I don't miss?"

She smiled.

"You may have anything you like."

"Anything?" he asked.

"Oh, yes," she said, "anything."

He pretended to consider the bet carefully, and then nodded.

"All right," he said, "you have a wager."

"Good," she said. "You can't possibly hit this cork while it's moving. It's too small."

"Just toss it high."

NINE

She smiled, brought her hand back, and tossed the cork into the air underhanded. It flew high, almost disappearing in the sunlight.

Clint squinted, pointed the gun, and fired. The cork leapt even higher in the air as his shot struck it, and then he fired again and again, causing the cork to dance in the air.

"Once more!" she shouted.

He had fired six shots already and had no time to reload. Swiftly, he transferred the big Colt to his left hand and drew the Colt New Line from behind him with the right. The cork was on its way down when he fired with the smaller gun, and it leapt once again before falling to the ground.

He turned and found Lillie staring at him with her mouth open.

"That's amazing!" she said.

"Thank you, ma'am."

"No," she said, "I'm serious. That last shot . . . how did you draw the other gun so fast?"

"The same way Annie Oakley makes all her trick shots," he said. "I was born with that ability."

"She is accurate," Lillie said, "but you, you are accurate and fast."

Clint ejected the spent shell from the New Line and replaced it with a live shell from his pocket. Then he did the same with the big Colt, ejecting the spent shells and replacing them with six more from his gun belt. That done, he slid the gun into the holster. He also tucked the smaller gun into his belt again, at the small of his back. He considered himself lucky that he had removed his jacket during the picnic. He might not have been able to draw the New Line in time if he'd still had the jacket on, and he would not have been able to impress Lillie.

He was surprised that he had found the trick shooting fun. He had not had fun with a gun in a very long time.

"Well," she said, "I suppose you want to collect on your wager."

"Of course," he said, "wouldn't you?"

"Certainly. I always collect when I win, and pay when I lose."

"Well, that's good."

"So tell me," she said, "what is it you want as payment?"

He smiled and pretended to think.

"Come, come," she said, "you must have . . . something in mind?"

"I do," he said.

"What?" From the look on her face he knew she thought she knew what it was.

"You," he finally said.

"Men," she said.

"Naked."

"You're all alike . . ."

"Now!"

"So predict—what?"

"You heard me," he said. "I want you naked, now. I want to make love to you."

"Here?"

"Here," he said, "and now."

"But . . ." she said, looking around. "We're in a public park."

He grinned and said, "The park is huge, and it will probably take them forever to find us."

She smiled back at him and said, "I know you're joking. This is a joke. Come, we can go back to my hotel, where there is a perfectly wonderful bed—"

"I'm not joking, Lillie."

She stopped, stared at him, and said, "You must be."

"I'm not."

"But—"

"You said I could have anything I wanted."

"Yes, but—"

"Anything."

She put her hands on her hips, looked around, then looked back at him.

"You said that you always pay your wagers."

"All right, damn you," she said, "you shall have your prize."

She started to undress.

TEN

The possibility of being caught in the park excited both of them.

He watched as she disrobed, his penis thickening inside his pants. He'd gotten himself into it now. If he was going to have her here, *he* was going to have to strip, as well.

When her breasts swayed into view, he could see that her nipples were already hard. The sun was warm, so that could only be from her excitement. He knew he was right when she stepped from her pile of clothing, completely naked. He could *smell* her readiness.

"Now you," she said breathlessly.

He undid his gun belt and dropped it to the ground.

"Not yet," he said, approaching her.

She stood very still as he undid her hair, letting it fall to her shoulders.

"I get the impression you don't like my hair up," she said.

"It's beautiful hair," he said. "It should be down."

"Are you going to undress?" she asked.

"Not yet," he said again, and moved around behind her.

Her buttocks were full, firm and round. Lillie Langtry was a woman built for sex, padded where she should be, slender in very few places.

He touched her pale, smooth skin, following the line of her back down to where it met her buttocks. Rarely had he ever seen anything as beautiful as the line of a woman's back, the swell of her buttocks.

He put his hands on her cheeks, sliding one finger down the crease between them, causing her to shudder.

"Are you cold?" he asked.

"No."

He continued down, getting on his knees so he could run his hands over her thighs and calves. With her ass directly in front of his face he couldn't resist. He leaned forward and kissed one cheek, then the other, then ran his tongue between them. She moaned and spread her legs a bit to accommodate him. He, in turn, placed his hands inside her thighs and spread her legs even further. He turned his back and then leaned between her legs so he was looking up at her pussy. He touched it first with his hand, running his middle finger along her slit, finding it wet. He reached up then with his tongue and ran the tip of it along her, just lightly tasting her. Her body jerked, as if prodded, and her legs trembled.

"Damn you . . ." she said.

"These are the spoils of our wager," he said, "collected as I see fit."

He placed his hands on both thighs and probed more deeply with his tongue. She groaned as he entered her, then as he withdrew and swirled his tongue around her.

"God . . ." she said, "I'm going to . . . oh, good Lord . . ."

She trembled as a wave of pleasure overcame her. It was a small one, but it was there. He felt it and smiled.

He slid through her legs so he was sitting in front of her and planted a kiss on her still trembling belly.

"Take off your clothes, damn it!" she said.

"Yes," he said, "it's time."

"It's *about* time!"

He stood up and began to undress, no longer worried about being seen. All he wanted to do now was plunge his raging penis inside of her.

"W-what," she stammered, "what if someone comes along?"

As naked as she now, he said, "Then they'll get quite a show, won't they, Lillie?"

"Yes," she said, as he laid her down on the blanket and mounted her. "Oh, yessss . . ."

The man watched from behind some bushes. Lillie was so beautiful he found himself holding his breath. He had never seen her naked before, and he thought that he might swoon. The only thing that kept him from doing so was his anger, which was directed at the man. *He* should be the one making love to Lillie Langtry, not this man. No one loved Lillie the way he did.

Soon, she would learn that.

ELEVEN

They made love on the blanket for a long time, enjoying each other's bodies, sweating so that even the slightest of breezes made them shiver. Finally, they dressed once again, unaware that they were being watched.

Lillie noticed that Clint's arm was bleeding, soaking through the bandage a bit.

"How is your arm?"

"It's fine," he said. "I barely feel it."

He finished closing his trousers and reached for his gun belt. As she put the finishing touches to her dress, a man suddenly came into view, wearing a blue uniform.

"What timing," Clint said as the policeman approached them.

Lillie put her hands up to touch her hair, then decided there was nothing she could do about it now.

The policeman reached them and eyed them suspiciously.

"Thought I heard shooting," he said.

"Just a little target shooting, Officer," Clint said.

"It's a public park, you know," the man said, his tone scolding them.

"We know that."

"Let's have no more shooting, then," the man said, with a slight Irish accent.

"We won't, Officer," Lillie said, "I promise."

The man looked at Lillie, after having properly eyed Clint up and down, and then his eyes widened.

"Why, faith," he said, "you're Lillie Langtry."

"I am flattered you recognize me."

"Flattered?" he said, shocked. "Dear lady, only a blind man would not be able to recognize the darlin' of the stage herself."

The man was in his fifties, safely within the age range where men were charmed by her. Clint judged that range to be roughly eight to eighty.

"You are too kind," Lillie said.

The man eyed their basket, and their blanket, and their disheveled appearance, and said, "I won't be botherin' yer picnic anymore, Miss Lillie."

"You're a kind man, Officer," she said. "I'll keep my companion from doing any more target shooting." Then she added with an Irish accent, "It's a show-off, he is."

"Faith and you're not Irish, are ya?" the man asked hopefully.

"No," she said, "but it's a beautiful language, isn't it?"

"Aye, that it is," the man said. "Good day to you, Miss Langtry." He tipped his hat.

"Good day, Officer."

As the policeman walked away, Clint looked at Lillie with admiration.

"You do it to them all, don't you?"

"You should know, Clint Adams," she said. "God, what shall I do with my hair? Can we go back to the hotel now?"

"I insist on it," he said.

"Oh? Do you think you still have a wager to collect on?"

"I don't think I need one" he said, "do you?"

"Faith and the man has a silver tongue, doesn't he?" she said.

TWELVE

Clint extended his stay two more days, but he was still ready to leave several days before Lillie was.

"I won't ask you to stay longer," she said, the morning he was to leave. They had spent that night at her hotel. They'd spent each of the nights together at her hotel because her room had a larger, softer bed. They had made love indoors every day since that day in the park.

"I'm taking you away from your adoring public," he said.

"Not at all," she said. "I'd rather spend the time with you."

He was dressing and she was watching him. He thought she took as much pleasure in watching him dress as he did her.

"Will you even remember me when you go back

home to your princes and kings?" he asked.

"I will always remember you," she said, "and I'm not going home from here. I am here for the year, to tour the United States, remember?"

"That's right." She had told him that. "Will you be doing the West?"

"Certainly," she said. "There are men there, aren't there?"

"Oh, yes," he said, "a lot of men, and they'll be real happy to see you."

He walked to the bed and took her lovely face in his hands. They had agreed that she would not see him to the train station. He had no doubt she'd be mobbed there.

He kissed her tenderly, and she put her hand on his right wrist.

"I understand the West is still somewhat wild and untamed," she said.

"You can call on me anytime you need me," he said. "I'll leave you a way to contact me." He wrote down Rick Hartman's address in Labyrinth, Texas. Rick always knew how to get in touch with him.

"I might do that," she said, rubbing his arm, "if I need you."

He kissed her again and said, "I have to go, Lillie. Thank you."

"For what?"

"For making my stay in New York a magic one."

"I should thank you," she said. "You kept me from being bored."

He laughed.

"Is that all I did?"

"No," she said seriously, "you did much more than

that, and I thank you, Clint Adams."

They kissed again, long and hard, and then she pushed him away.

"Go," she said, "before I make a fool of myself, which I have never done before with a man."

He walked to the door, then turned and looked at her on the bed.

"Soon, Lillie," he said.

She smiled and said, "Soon, my Gunsmith."

It was the first time in a long time someone had called him that and it didn't make him flinch.

The man who had attacked Clint Adams, and spied on him and Lillie in the park, followed Clint to Grand Central Station, where he would be catching a train west. The man was pleased to see that Clint was leaving. Having found out who he was by asking at Clint's hotel, he had decided not to try to attack him again— at least not by himself. It would be foolish to do so, considering the man's reputation. He counted himself lucky to have been able to wound the man and escape earlier in the week.

He had explored other options, such as hiring someone, but then it occurred to him that Clint Adams and Lillie Langtry might be going their separate ways soon. He'd decided to wait until the end of the week to see what would happen, and, sure enough, Clint Adams was getting on a train.

From this day forward, he thought as Clint's train pulled out of the station, Lillie Langtry would be his.

THIRTEEN

Eight Months Later

When Clint got word from Rick Hartman that Lillie Langtry was trying to get in touch with him, he couldn't help but think back to that week they had spent together in New York. He smiled as he remembered their wager, and how she had ultimately paid him right there in Central Park. If that policeman had come by any sooner he would have certainly gotten an eyeful.

Clint had been in Arizona when he got Rick's message that Lillie was in Denver and wanted to see him. Actually, what Rick had said was that Lillie needed his help. Clint, having left the rig behind in Labyrinth, was able to ride Duke directly to Denver and arrived there within three days of getting Lillie's message.

He had sent a telegram ahead, addressing it to her at the theater she was playing. It had simply said: "I'm on my way."

Clint had been to Denver many times, and the Denver House was a hotel that he had stayed at before.

"Mr. Adams," the desk clerk said, "it's nice to see you back."

Clint remembered the clerk, but not the man's name.

"Thank you."

"How did you arrive, sir?"

"My horse is outside."

"Ah, I'll have one of the boys take your horse to our livery."

"Tell him to be careful not to lose any fingers," Clint said.

"Ah, yes, well, perhaps I'll have the liveryman come around and get the animal himself."

"That might be a good idea."

"How long are you planning to stay this time?" the man asked.

"I don't know," Clint said. "This trip was sort of spur-of-the-moment."

"Hmmm. Luggage?"

"Just my saddlebags," Clint said, which were slung over his shoulder.

"Shall I have someone show you to your room?"

"Just let me have a key," Clint said. "I can find my way."

"Do you still prefer a room overlooking the street?" the man asked.

"Yes."

"Very well, sir." The clerk gave him a key and said, "Enjoy your stay."

"Thank you."

"Uh, one hopes there won't be any trouble this trip . . . will there?"

Clint gave the man a humorless smile and said, "One never knows, does one?"

Up in his room Clint dropped the saddlebags on the bed and walked to the window. He'd been following Lillie's progress through the newspapers. She had become the darling of America as well as Europe, and of late—the past few months—she had been conquering the West. Even Dodge City had been charmed by her. Now she was in Denver, working her magic there.

If things seemed to be going so right for her, though, why did she need his help?

He would have come to Denver even if she had sent word that she simply wanted to see him. The sights, sounds, and tastes of Lillie Langtry were still with him, even after eight months. Also, the force of her personality. The fact that she was asking for help was a cause for great concern.

Clint had to go downstairs to buy a newspaper. When he had it he went to the dining room, ordered lunch, and opened the paper. The first thing he looked for was anything about Lillie. She was playing at the Denver Palace, and according to the paper she was playing to a packed house every night.

Since Lillie had not left word with Rick as to where she was staying, Clint knew that he was going to have to go to the Denver Palace if he wanted to see

her. He decided to waste no time and go that very
night.

He was impatient to know what was bothering Lillie Langtry so much that she had to send word to him
for help.

FOURTEEN

Lillie Langtry stared at herself in the mirror. She thought she looked a fright. There were lines at the corners of her eyes, and she knew they were worry lines that had not been there eight months before when she had first come to this country.

She wondered when Clint Adams would arrive. The telegram he had sent to the theater had indicated he was leaving immediately for Denver. The dear, sweet man had not even asked for an explanation.

What could she have told him? How could she convey in a telegram how frightened she truly was?

The knock on the door made her start, and she put a hand to her throat.

"Yes?"

"It's me, Lillie."

Anson Schepp, her manager.

"Come in."

The door opened and the tall, distinguished-looking, white-haired man entered and closed it quietly behind him.

"You startled me," she said.

"I'm sorry," he said. "I had to knock. If I had just entered . . ."

"I know," she said, waving his apology away. "I'm being silly."

He approached her and looked at her in the mirror. "You look lovely."

"I look a fright."

"You've never looked a fright in your life."

She smiled at him and said, "You're sweet."

When Lillie had started to perform she had been approached immediately by Anson. He insisted she needed someone to handle the "mundane" details, and he had been right. Anson made all of her bookings, all of her travel arrangements, hotel accommodations. He handled all of the details she hated to think about. He also negotiated her fees for her performances, and he had been doing a marvelous job at that.

"It'll be all right," he said, putting his hands on her shoulders.

As much as she liked Anson and appreciated all he had done for her, she found that she was uncomfortable with his touch. She quelled the urge to shake his hands off and concentrated on putting makeup on her face, trying to hide the lines.

"I am fine," she said.

Anson knew how frightened she was, but they did not talk about it. Or rather, *she* did not talk about it.

She only wanted to discuss it with Clint Adams.

How odd, she thought. She had known the man for less than a week in New York, and yet he was the only one she could think to turn to. She knew there were any number of men in Europe who would hurry to her side to protect her, but she never even considered contacting them. It was Clint Adams who had come immediately to mind . . . for a lot of reasons.

Not the least of which was that he was a deadly shot with a gun.

Schepp, seeing that Lillie did not want to talk, removed his hands from her shoulders and backed away.

"I'll wait for you outside," he said.

"All right, Anson."

"You'll be wonderful tonight, Lillie," he said. "You always are."

Like most men Anson was a little in love with Lillie. Sometimes, though, he thought of her as a daughter, and that was the way he felt tonight.

"Thank you, Anson."

"Well . . . I'll let you finish."

He backed his way to the door, then slipped out and closed it gently.

Lillie stopped what she was doing, dropped her hands into her lap, and stared into the mirror.

Where was Clint Adams?

And would *he* be out there tonight?

Out in the hall Anson Schepp was approached by Charles Kendall, the manager of the Denver Palace.

"How is she?" the little man asked, wringing his hands.

"She'll be fine."

"Is she happy with her dressing room?"

"It's fine."

"Is there enough light?"

"There's plenty, Mr. Kendall, stop worrying."

"I just want her to be happy, Mr. Schepp."

That was what most men wanted, Schepp thought, but why was it only most men? Why not all?

"Mr. Kendall," he said, putting his arm around the smaller man's shoulders, "can we talk about security?"

"Why do we need security?" the manager asked nervously, as Anson Schepp led him away from Lillie Langtry's dressing room.

Out in the audience one man waited even more anxiously than the rest for the appearance of Lillie Langtry. She knew about him now, knew that he wanted to take care of her.

Knew that he loved her as no other man could.

He smiled, looking around at the predominantly male audience. There were women there, too, but their men were not paying attention to them. They were all gazing at the stage, waiting for the appearance of his darling Lillie.

None of them knew that she belonged to him.

FIFTEEN

Clint arrived at the Denver Palace a few minutes before the show was supposed to start. Since he doubted he would be able to get a seat up front at this late date, he wanted to enter and stand in the back, hoping that Lillie might see him that way. After the show he would try to get backstage to see her, or get word to her that he was there.

"Would you like a seat, sir?" an usher asked him. "There are a few left."

"No, thank you," Clint said. "I prefer to stand back here."

"Very well, sir," the man said, eyeing him suspiciously. "Enjoy the show."

"Thank you, I will."

The uniformed usher moved away, but Clint noticed that he did not go far and was keeping an eye on him. Did this have anything to do with Lillie's "trouble"? he wondered.

If there had been a few seats left, they were no longer available when the curtain went up and Lillie Langtry stood center stage.

She looked and sounded beautiful, and Clint now realized that there was no way she was going to notice him, since the back of the theater was in shadows. He would just have to wait until the show was over to try to get backstage to see her.

The show was almost over when Clint felt a presence behind him. He turned and saw two men. One was tall and white-haired, and the other shorter, with brown hair and muttonchops. Behind them stood the usher.

Clint felt sure the man with the muttonchops was a policeman.

"Sir?" the man asked. "May we ask what you're doing back here?"

"I'm enjoying the show."

"The usher tells me that you had an opportunity to get a seat."

"I didn't want a seat."

"Why not?"

"Because I'd rather stand."

"May I ask—"

"May I ask who you are?" Clint interrupted the man.

"Certainly, sir." The man took out his badge. "My name is Lieutenant Hathaway. And you are?"

"Clint Adams."

The policeman looked surprised; he obviously recognized the name.

So did the white-haired man.

"Wait a minute," he said. "You're Clint Adams?"

"That's right."

"It's all right, Lieutenant," the man said. "Mr. Adams is a friend of Miss Langtry."

"All right, sir," the policeman said. "If you vouch for him."

"I do."

"Sorry to have bothered you, sir," Hathaway said to Clint.

"That's all right."

The policeman moved away and left, and the white-haired man turned to Clint and put out his hand.

"I'm Anson Schepp."

Clint took the man's hand.

"You're Lillie's manager."

"That's right. We didn't get a chance to meet in New York, but Lillie told me a lot about you."

"Did she?" Clint wondered just how much Lillie had told her manager.

"Yes, indeed. What brings you to Denver, Mr. Adams?"

"Lillie does," Clint said. "She sent word that she wanted to see me."

"Ah," Schepp said, "now I understand."

"Well, that's good," Clint said, "because I don't. Maybe you can explain it to me?"

"I think I'll let Lillie do that," Schepp said. "Come with me. She's almost done, and we can meet her backstage."

Clint followed the man out into the lobby, and then through a door marked PRIVATE. It led to a hallway, and then a stairway, and Clint assumed it would ultimately lead backstage.

"When did the police get involved in theater security?" Clint asked.

"Today," Schepp said. "I asked the manager to talk to them, and they sent the lieutenant and a few men."

"The usher?"

Schepp nodded.

"There are a few ushers who are actually policemen, yes."

"Is Lillie in danger?"

"She thinks she is."

"And you don't?"

Schepp hesitated before answering.

"Let's just say I haven't seen any evidence of it, but whether she is or not, she's worried, or she wouldn't have sent for you."

They finally reached the backstage area, and Clint was able to get a closer look at Lillie onstage. She was breathtaking. Leaning forward he was able to see the faces of the people in the audience who were sitting up close. Men and women both seemed enraptured by Lillie's performance. If anything, Clint thought she was even better than she had been in New York eight months earlier. Unfortunately, these musicians were not as good as the ones in New York—or maybe they were. What did he know about music, anyway?

She finished her last song and the house erupted. People stood and applauded. Lillie took her bows, then turned and came offstage. She didn't see him at first until her manager pointed him out.

"Lillie," Schepp said, "look who's here."

She turned, saw Clint, and flung herself into his arms.

"Oh, I'm so glad you've come. I've been frantic!"

"Uh, Miss Langtry?"

Clint looked past Lillie at the man who was trying to get her attention.

"Miss Langtry?" he said again. "They want you to come back out."

"What?" She turned and looked at the man. "Oh." She looked at Clint.

"Go ahead," he said. "I'll be right here."

"We have to talk," she said.

"That's what I'm here for."

She smiled at him and said, "I hope that's not all you're here for."

Clint laughed as she went back out onto the stage. Whatever the problem was, Lillie had not lost her sense of humor.

SIXTEEN

After Lillie took her extra bows, she grabbed both of Clint's hands and dragged him into her dressing room. The first thing she did was kiss him soundly, and then hug him tightly.

"What's wrong, Lillie?"

She released him and sat down. He remained standing.

"I'm frightened."

"I find that hard to believe."

"So do I."

"What are you afraid of?"

"A man."

"I find that even harder to believe," he said. "Who's the man?"

"I don't know."

"What does he look like?"

"I don't know."

"Have you ever seen him?"

"No."

"How do you know he's there?"

"He spoke to me."

"When?"

"Last week."

"Where?"

"We were in Kansas City," she said. "It was after my last performance. I went back to my room and . . . and he was there."

"And you didn't see him?"

"It was dark, and he wouldn't let me turn up the lamp."

"What did he do?"

"He didn't . . . do anything. He talked to me."

"About what?"

"He said he loved me," she said. "He said that he'd been with me all during my tour. He said that he had seen us in New York."

That got Clint's attention.

"He mentioned me?"

She nodded.

"By name," she said.

"Did he say anything about the attack on me?"

"No, not specifically."

"All right," he said, "go on. What else did he have to say?"

"A lot," she said. "He just talked and talked and talked. I don't remember most of it."

"How long was he in your room, Lillie?"

"Hours," she said. "All night. He left before it got light."

"Did you talk to the law?"

"No."

"Why not?"

"What could I tell them?" she asked. "I didn't see him, I can't identify him."

"Do you believe what he said?"

"About what?"

"That he's been with you throughout your tour?"

She nodded.

"He said he's been in the audience for every performance, Clint."

"And he did mention me in New York," he said. "Have you heard from him here?"

"No," she said, "but I haven't been able to sleep much since Kansas City." She touched her face. "I'm starting to look my age."

"Oh, yes," he said, "you look every day of twenty-nine, Lillie."

"No," she said, "I look older."

She turned and looked in the mirror, then turned away from him.

"He's ruining me," she said. "I find myself wanting to go back to England."

"Has he said anything about being there?"

She looked shocked, as if she hadn't ever considered that.

"I think we better get out of here and talk someplace else," he said, "someplace more private."

"Where?"

"Leave that to me," he said. "Put something on and let's go."

SEVENTEEN

Clint took Lillie, wrapped in a shawl, to his hotel. Although the people in the lobby couldn't recognize her face, it was difficult to hide her figure, and they attracted attention anyway.

The only person they'd spoken to when they left the theater was her manager, Anson Schepp.

"We have to go someplace and talk privately, Anson," Lillie had told him.

Clint thought the man looked hurt, but he said, "Just don't disappear on me, Lillie, dear. I'd be terribly upset if that happened."

"I won't disappear, Anson."

When they reached the hotel Clint took her directly into the dining room. He called a waiter over and gave him five dollars.

"I need a *very* private table."

"That can be arranged, sir."

The waiter brought out a partition and took them to a corner table. When he spread the screen in front of them, they had all the privacy they'd need.

"Are you hungry?" Clint asked.

"Famished," she said. "I'm always hungry after a performance."

Clint ordered coffee for both of them, and then they each ordered a steak dinner.

"Lillie," he said, when the waiter left with their order, "tell me again everything that happened in Kansas City. As much as you can remember, word for word, of what he said."

She tried. She closed her eyes and tried to picture the scene in the hotel room. . . .

As she entered her room, he came up behind her before she could turn the lamp up.

"Hello, Lillie, my darling," he said in her ear. "I've been waiting for you. It's time we met."

His breath was hot on her neck, but not like a lover's. He smelled of garlic, and of rotted teeth, and it was all she could do to keep from gagging.

"Don't you have anything to say?" he asked.

"W-who are you?"

"I'm the man who loves you, Lillie," he said. "The *only* man who *really* loves you. Not like all those fools who watch you on the stage. Not like all those men who use you and then cast you aside. Not like men like Clint Adams . . ."

"He mentioned me by name?" Clint asked, interrupting her.

She opened her eyes and looked at him, astonished that she had remembered that.

"Yes, he did."

"What else did he say about me—wait, never mind that. Close your eyes and go back. Just give it to me in order."

She closed her eyes and began talking again. . . .

". . . in New York. He didn't love you like I do, did he?"

She didn't answer. She didn't *have* an answer.

"Are you going to hurt me?" she asked.

"Why would I hurt you, my darling?" the man asked. "When I just told you that I love you."

"W-what do you want?"

"I just wanted us to meet."

"I-I can't see you."

"This will do nicely for now," he said. "I want you to sit down. I'll lead you to a chair, all right?"

"It's dark."

"That's all right," he said, "I can see in the dark. Are you ready? Here we go."

From behind, with his hands on her, he steered her to a chair and sat her down. Then he pulled a chair over and sat down just behind her.

"There," he said, "now we can have a nice visit. . . ."

"He stayed most of the night," she said, "and after he left I couldn't move for almost half an hour. I was afraid that he might still be in the room."

"What else did he say, Lillie?"

She opened her eyes.

"I don't want to remember it this way anymore," she said. "It's like he's still there, sitting behind me, breathing on me."

He decided not to force her.

"All right," he said, "just tell me what else you remember."

"Just that he said he's been with me since New York, and he'll always be with me. He said that I will learn to love him."

"And if you don't?"

"He didn't say."

"And you haven't heard from him since?"

"Not directly," she said, "but every performance since Kansas City I receive a bouquet of flowers."

"From who?"

"It never says. They're from him, though. I know it." She wrinkled her nose and said, "They even smell like him. God! I can't get that odor out of my nostrils."

"Maybe this will help," Clint said as the waiter arrived with their food.

The aroma of the cooked meat filled the air, mingling with that of the coffee. Clint found that he, too, was very hungry.

"I'm afraid, Clint," she said as they began to eat. "How did he get into my hotel room? And he's in the theater every night."

"Do you believe that?"

"Yes, I do. He knows too much about each performance. He knows that we had some difficulty with one of the musicians in Chicago. It held up the show for an hour. He knows too many things not to have been there."

"And he knows about me," Clint said, "so he was in New York."

"He's the man who attacked you."

"Did he say that?"

"No," she said, "but he must be, don't you think?"

Clint shrugged.

"You didn't see him, I didn't see him," he said. "The man seems to be a ghost of some kind."

Lillie shivered.

EIGHTEEN

After dinner Clint had some coffee, Lillie had a cup of tea.

"What do you want to do now?" Clint asked.

"I don't know," she said. "I don't want to cancel the rest of my tour."

"Where do you go after this?"

"California."

"Where in California?"

She thought a moment.

"Sacramento, San Francisco . . . and a couple of other places. Anson does the bookings, he would know."

"Have you talked to Anson about this?"

"No."

"Why not?"

She hesitated, then said, "I'm not sure."

"Do you trust him?"

"I do . . . up to a point. I trust him to make my arrangements."

"Your performing arrangements?"

"And traveling arrangements."

"But nothing else?"

She shrugged.

"Why?"

She looked at Clint and said, "He is a man. I trust very few men, Clint."

"I'm flattered."

"You should be," she said. "I told you once that men were easy to control. That does not make them likeable, or trustworthy."

"So I'm the only one you've told?"

"Yes."

"What does Anson know?"

"Only that I have been upset about a man."

"But he doesn't know that the man was in your room."

"No."

"You should have told him, Lillie," Clint said, "so he could arrange protection."

"That's what I want you to do."

"I can arrange it. In fact, I know someone right here in Denver—"

"No, I don't want you to arrange it," she said, cutting him off, "I want you to protect me."

He studied her for a moment and said, "I can do that, but what happens when you leave Denver?"

"Clint," she said, "I want you to come with me. I want you to protect me the rest of the time I'm in America."

Travel around with her for the rest of her tour? That would mean putting his own life on hold. But they were friends, and she was in danger—or, at least, she thought she was.

"Will you do it?"

"What will you tell Anson?"

"That I want you to travel with us."

"Will that be all right with him?"

She smiled and said, "He's a man, Clint. Whatever I want is all right with him."

Clint sat back.

"Tell me about Anson."

"What about him?"

"Just tell me what you know."

She told him how they met in England, how he convinced her that she needed a manager.

"Did he have any experience?"

"He said he did."

"But you don't know for sure?"

"I've never spoken to anyone he's managed before, if that's what you mean."

That was what he meant.

"You don't suspect Anson—it wasn't Anson in my room, Clint."

"I know that, Lillie," Clint said. "I'm just asking questions, is all."

"Will you help me, Clint?"

"Of course I'll help you, Lillie," he said. "I told you back in New York if you ever needed me I'd be there—and here I am."

NINETEEN

After they finished eating Clint suggested that he take Lillie back to her hotel.

"I thought I would stay here, with you."

"That would drive your manager crazy, wouldn't it?" he asked. "No, I think we should go back to your hotel."

"Will you stay there with me?"

"Sure." He couldn't think of a reason not to, and there were a lot of reasons to go ahead and do it.

They went out in front of his hotel and had the doorman get them a cab, then went directly to her hotel.

The man across the street from Lillie's hotel could not believe his eyes. He watched as Lillie was helped out of the cab by the doorman, and then a man got out after her—and it was Clint Adams!

The last time he had seen Clint Adams was in New York, getting on a train, and he had never expected to see him again. Now here he was, in Denver, with Lillie again.

He felt the anger boil up inside of him. Hadn't he visited Lillie in her room, professed his love, and spent time with her? How could she do this to him now?

He was so angry he didn't know how to react, and before he knew it Lillie and Clint Adams had entered her hotel. Now all he could do was wait and see when Clint Adams came out.

Just in walking from the cab to the hotel door Clint stayed alert. He didn't want to be surprised the way he had been in New York.

"What is it?" Lillie asked.

"I'm just being careful, Lillie," he said.

She put her hand on his arm and said, "I feel better already."

In the lobby they were met by a frantic Anson Schepp.

"Where have you been, my dear? I've been so worried."

Clint hadn't noticed Schepp's English accent so much earlier. Apparently it grew thicker the more frightened he got.

"We just went to dinner, Anson," she said. "We haven't even been gone that long."

"Well . . . I'm just glad you're back. Would you like me to walk you to your room?"

"There's no need," she said. "Clint will walk me."

"Oh . . . very well. I'm sure you'll be safe with Mr. Adams."

"Anson, you better start calling him Clint."

"Why is that?"

"Because he's going to be around for the rest of the tour."

"The rest—you mean the rest of your time here in Denver, don't you?"

"No," she said, "I mean the rest of our time here in America."

"I see."

Schepp's face and tone betrayed nothing, and yet Clint still got the impression the man wasn't very happy about this decision.

"In what capacity will he be traveling with us?" he asked.

"Security."

"Well . . . good, then. If that will make you feel calmer about things, then I'm all for it."

"Why don't you get some rest, Anson?" Lillie suggested. "You look like you could use it. You've been worrying about me too much."

"That's my job, my dear," he said. "To worry about you and look after you."

"Well," Lillie said, "that's Clint's job now. You can just concentrate on traveling arrangements and bookings."

"Uh . . . yes, of course."

"And you'd better see to Clint's comfort wherever we go from now on. We'll need another room."

"Yes," Schepp said, "I'll see to it."

"Good night, Anson."

As they walked up the steps Clint said, "He didn't

seem too happy with the new arrangement."

"He'll have to get used to it."

As they continued up the steps Clint had the feeling that Anson Schepp was watching their backs, but he didn't turn around to check.

TWENTY

When they made love this time he found her almost desperate. He tried to slow her down, but she would have none of it.

"I'm very frightened," she told him, "and you're here and you make me feel safe, but I need to get rid of some of the fear that's still inside of me."

"This way?"

She laughed and said, "Can you think of a better way to exhaust yourself?"

She turned him over onto his back then and fell on him, her mouth hot and avid. She covered his body with kisses from head to toe, and then with bites along the inside of his thigh, and finally took his rigid penis into her mouth. She moaned and sighed as she sucked him wetly, and when he could take no more he had to forcibly remove himself from her mouth.

He turned her onto her back then and did the same thing to her, except that when he attacked her with his mouth she was not strong enough to push him away—nor did she want to. She arched her back and wailed as his tongue continued to lash at her, and then he mounted her and entered her forcefully.

She wrapped herself around him and they strained at each other, lunging so hard that the bed actually moved several times.

Later they lay together, exhausted, and she said, "Oh, God, I needed that."

"You could have your pick of any man if you needed to exhaust yourself."

She took his hand, squeezed, and said, "I needed to exhaust myself with you, Clint Adams."

He leaned over and kissed her.

"I'm so grateful to you for coming," she said. "I can't tell you how much."

"You don't have to," he said. "How many more performances do you have here in Denver?"

"Two," she said, "one tomorrow night, and a matinee the day after. We leave the day after that."

"To go where?"

"Sacramento, I think, but you'd have to check with Anson."

He tossed the sheet back and swung his feet to the floor.

"Where are you going?"

They were in a two-room suite, so he said, "If I'm going to spend the night here I want to make sure the room is secure before we go to sleep."

She laughed and asked, "What makes you think we're going to sleep?"

"Well," he said, "eventually."

The man across the street finally admitted to himself that Clint Adams wasn't coming out.

He wished now that he had succeeded in killing Adams in New York. Now he was just going to have to take care of it here.

Anson Schepp stood down the hall from Lillie Langtry's room, staring at the closed door. He was waiting for it to open, for Clint Adams to come out and walk down the hall, but he knew that wasn't going to happen.

He closed his own door and locked it, then sighed and went to sit on the bed. All right, he was Lillie's manager, not her protector. That role would now fall to Clint Adams. That was the way Lillie wanted it, and that was fine with Anson.

After all, he only wanted the best for Lillie, didn't he?

TWENTY-ONE

In the morning Clint was awakened by a knock on the door.

"That will be breakfast," Lillie said sleepily. "I always have it brought to the room."

"I'll get the door."

Clint got up and opened the door, admitting the bellboy. He tipped the boy, and as he was closing the door behind him Lillie came out of the other room, belting a robe around her waist. She came up to him, pressed herself against him, and kissed him.

"Good morning."

"Morning," he said. "What time is it?"

"Eight A.M.," she said. "That's when I have breakfast brought in."

"I guess I should see about getting myself some breakfast."

80

"No need."

She disengaged herself from him and walked to the breakfast tray.

"I always order more than I can eat," she said, whisking the top off the tray. "There's plenty here."

And there was. There was ham and eggs and potatoes for more than two people, along with biscuits and coffee.

They sat down and ate breakfast together, sitting across from each other.

"What is your schedule today?" he asked.

"Nothing until the show tonight," she said. "I hadn't planned on leaving my room."

"I might go out for a little while."

"What for?"

"To see a friend."

"Who?"

"A detective."

"Why?"

"It strikes me as foolish just to sit and wait for this man to make a move on you again, Lillie. I just thought I might enlist some help in trying to find him."

"I will come with you."

"Why? You could stay here—"

"I'm too frightened to stay alone any longer," she said. "I would like to come with you."

"All right," he said. "How long will it take you to get ready?"

She smiled at him and said, "What a silly question. Hours!"

"See if you can keep it down to two," he said.

"A lady can't rush her bath, Clint," she said, "especially if there's a gentleman in it with her."

They didn't get out of the room until noon.

Talbot Roper and Clint Adams owed each other so many favors they had lost count. That's why Clint had no qualms about asking for one.

When Clint and Lillie entered Roper's office, his young secretary stood up and stared at them, wide-eyed.

Actually, she was staring at Lillie.

"Y-you're Lillie Langtry."

"That's right."

"I—I—I saw you last night. You were magnificent."

"Why, thank you."

"Is Roper in?" Clint asked.

The girl continued to stare at Lillie.

"You're even more beautiful up close," she said.

"How very sweet of you to say," Lillie said. "Is Mr. Roper in?"

"Uh, yes, I'll tell him you're here."

"Tell him I'm here, too," Clint said.

The girl looked at him and frowned.

"Clint Adams."

"Oh," she said, putting her hands over her mouth. "Mr. Adams. Sure, he's mentioned you. I'll tell him."

As the girl left the room, Clint turned to Lillie, who looked amused.

"He always seems to have a new secretary."

"I see."

When the girl reappeared Roper was right on her tail. He was a tall, distinguished-looking man about Clint's age, but at the moment he looked like a wide-

eyed schoolboy. It was a look Clint had never seen
before.

"By God, it is you," he said. "I thought she was
kidding me."

"It's me, Tal," Clint said.

"Not you," Roper said. "I was talking about Miss
Langtry." He looked at her again and said, "It really
is you."

"Does your secretary often lie to you, Mr. Roper,
about your guests?"

"Uh, no, of course not."

Lillie looked at the young woman and asked,
"What's your name?"

"Uh, Belle, ma'am. I mean, uh, my real name's Arabella. But everyone just calls me Belle."

"How silly," Lillie said. "Arabella is much too
pretty a name to be shortened."

"It is?"

"Oh, my, yes," Lillie said. "I shall call you Arabella—with your permission, of course."

"Uh, sure, of course," the girl said.

"Miss Langtry?" Roper said. "Would you like to
come into my office?"

"Thank you, Mr. Roper."

Roper ushered Lillie in past him, then turned and
said to Clint, "You, too," and followed her in.

"Gee, thanks," Clint said, bringing up the rear.

TWENTY-TWO

Roper made a fuss over Lillie, helping her with her chair, before seating himself behind the desk. It amused Clint to see the usually unflappable ladies' man so flustered by the beautiful Lillie.

Finally, Roper turned to Clint and shook his hand.

"Good to see you," he said.

"Nice of you to notice I was in the room."

"Well, can you blame me?" Roper asked. "Look at her. She's beautiful."

"Yes, she is," Clint said.

"You're both sweet."

"I have tickets to see you perform tonight," Roper told her.

"That's good," Clint said, "because that's where we want you."

Roper looked at Clint and said, "Oh no you don't.

84

I'm going there to enjoy the performance, not to work."

"I—we need a favor," Clint said.

"We truly need your help, Mr. Roper."

Clint could see that Roper was sunk. The detective sat behind his desk and said, "Tell me about it."

Clint made a brief tale of it, while still managing to convey the horror that Lillie felt, especially that night in Kansas City.

"So you see what we're up against."

Roper nodded.

"A nameless, faceless man."

"How do you find someone like that?" Lillie asked.

"Well," Roper said, "you put a name and a face to him."

"Can you do that?"

Roper smiled.

"I can try." He looked at Clint. "And what are you going to be doing while I'm trying that?"

"I'll be sticking close by Lillie."

Roper fixed him with a hard stare.

"Care to trade jobs?"

Clint smiled and said, "Nope."

"Didn't think so."

"How will you start to find him?" Lillie asked.

"I have some friends in Kansas City," Roper said. "We can start there."

"But . . . I didn't see him."

"Maybe somebody else did. You never know until you ask."

"We'd better go and let him get started," Clint said.

"Where can I get in touch with you?" Roper asked.

Clint gave him the name of Lillie's hotel.

"And your hotel?"

"For the time being," Clint said, "you can contact me at her hotel, also."

Roper's eyes—behind Lillie's back—told Clint he was a lucky son of a bitch.

"And how long do I have to perform this magic that I do?" Roper asked.

"We'll be leaving day after tomorrow," Clint said, "but I'll let you know where we are in California."

"But we will be seeing you at the performance tonight, won't we?" Lillie asked, turning to face Roper when they were in the outer office.

"I wouldn't miss it."

"And bring Arabella," Lillie said, looking at the young secretary.

Roper hesitated, then said, "I'll do that."

"Good. I will leave a ticket for her at the box office, and then I will leave word that you are to be allowed backstage afterward."

"Really?" Arabella said excitedly.

"Yes," Lillie said, "really. See you tonight."

Outside Clint said to Lillie, "That was a nice thing for you to do."

"What was?"

"Telling Roper to bring Arabella."

"Oh, Clint," she said. "Sometimes men are so naive. He would have brought her anyway. I just made it easier for him."

"What do you mean?" Clint asked. "You mean Talbot and Arabella . . ."

"It's so very easy to see."

"But . . . she's so much younger than he is."

"Women like older men," Lillie said, "and older men like younger women. It all balances out in the end, don't you think?"

TWENTY-THREE

The man was frantic.

He was standing across the street from Lillie's hotel, worriedly looking up and down the block. This had never happened before, in all the time he'd been watching Lillie. She and Clint Adams had come out of the hotel about noon and gotten right into a cab. He hadn't been able to get a cab quickly enough, and they had gotten away from him.

He'd lost her!

All he could do after that was find a doorway and wait for them to get back. But what if they didn't come back? What if she told Adams about him and he took her away somewhere?

What would he do then?

What would he do without Lillie?

He thought about going inside to ask if Lillie Langtry had checked out, but he doubted they would tell him anything. Besides, she hadn't taken any luggage with her—but maybe that was a trick.

Somehow he had to find out what had happened—and that was when the other man came out of the hotel.

He was tall and white-haired, and the man knew that he was Lillie's manager. If anyone would know where she was, he would.

He gave the man a half a block lead, then crossed and started to follow him.

Anson Schepp had no idea that he was being followed. He was on his way to the Denver Palace to make sure that everything was in order for the performance tonight. It was close enough to walk, and he enjoyed a brisk walk every day. It kept him young.

He was still several blocks from the Palace when he felt a hand on his back, and suddenly he was stumbling forward, trying to keep his balance. Before he could fall or right himself, someone grabbed him by the collar and yanked him into a nearby alley, where he was finally allowed to stagger and fall to the ground.

Because he sometimes carried large sums of money, Anson carried a small hide-out gun that fit in his jacket pocket. He was grabbing for it now when someone kicked him in the jaw. Everything began to spin as he fell onto his back. He was still conscious, and felt someone relieve him of the small gun. He knew he should have gotten a holster for the damned thing.

Before he could fully regain his senses someone

sat him up and knelt behind him. The man pulled him tightly against him and then put the point of a knife to his throat.

"Are you awake?"

"Huh?"

The man shook him and suddenly everything came into focus.

"Can you hear me?"

"Uh . . . yes."

"And understand me?"

It was hard to speak because his jaw was swollen from the kick.

"Yuh . . ."

"I'll take that as a yes. I have some questions for you, and I want you to answer them truthfully, okay?"

"Yeah . . ."

"If I don't like your answers I'll prick you, like this. . . ."

Anson jumped as the point of the knife dug into his skin.

"I'll do that three times," the man said, "and if I still don't like your answers I'll cut your throat. Understand?"

"But wai—"

The man pricked him again and he fell silent. He was so frightened his eyes were tearing uncontrollably.

"Now, are we ready?"

Anson found himself surprised at the man's voice. It was cultured, educated. This was no mere street robbery.

"Are we ready?" the man asked again, more forcefully.

"Yes, yes," Anson said, "I'm ready."

"Good," the man said, "first question . . ."

TWENTY-FOUR

When Clint and Lillie returned to the hotel there was some commotion in the lobby.

"What is happening?" she asked.

"I don't know."

As they got further inside Clint saw the policeman, Lieutenant Hathaway. He looked at them and waved a hand, as if to say, "There you are!"

"Officer!" he shouted to someone. "They're here."

A uniformed policeman waved to him, and then called out to some other uniformed men.

Hathaway came over to Clint and Lillie.

"Is something wrong, Lieutenant?" Lillie asked.

"Miss Langtry," Hathaway said, removing his hat, "if you would, I'd like you to return to your room with one of my officers."

"But why—"

92

"I have reason to think that your life might be in danger."

"But . . . that's why I have Mr. Adams with me," Lillie said, touching Clint for reassurance.

"I'm afraid I have to take Mr. Adams somewhere with me," Hathaway said. "Please, I would like your cooperation just now."

Lillie looked at Clint, and he nodded and said, "Go ahead, Lillie. I'll be back soon."

Hathaway called a man over who looked at Lillie, awestruck.

"This is Officer Banks," Hathaway said. "Please go with him."

"M-miss Langtry," Banks said. He was in his thirties, but his voice cracked when he said her name.

As the officer led Lillie to the stairway, Clint turned to look at Lieutenant Hathaway.

"What is it?" he asked. "What's happened?"

"I think you should come with me and see."

"But—" Clint said, unable to continue as Hathaway walked away.

The lieutenant walked Clint about three blocks from the hotel until they reached an alley.

"I'll assume you have a strong stomach."

"Strong enough."

"Come with me."

He led them further into the alley to where a circle of men were standing around something that was covered.

"Remove it," he told one of the men.

A uniformed policeman leaned over and removed the blanket that was covering . . . something.

"Do you know him?"

Clint moved closer and realized he was looking at a body. It was so covered with blood that he hadn't immediately recognized it as such. Now he could see that it was a man, and that parts of his body had been flayed from him, like a skinned deer. The face, however, was intact, and he could see that it was Anson Schepp.

"Oh, God . . ." he said, and wondered what he was going to tell Lillie.

"What can you tell me about this, Mr. Adams?" Hathaway asked.

They were standing outside the alley, the body having just been removed and taken to a nearby morgue.

"Not much."

"Obviously Miss Langtry is fearful of someone, probably the person who did this," Hathaway said. "If that were not the case, then I would not have been called to the theater last night. Correct?"

"I suppose."

The lieutenant took a moment to light a cigarette. Clint could see that the man's hands were shaking, though he wasn't sure of the cause. It could have been shock, or anger.

"I'm not getting the answers from you that I want, Mr. Adams," he said finally. "Why is that?"

"Lieutenant," Clint said, "if you're waiting for me to tell you who did this, I can't."

"I want you to tell me what you know, Mr. Adams," Hathaway said, "nothing more, and nothing less, and I want you to do it here, not at police headquarters."

"All right, Lieutenant, here's what I know," Clint said. He told the policeman about Lillie being visited in her room in Kansas City by someone who held her there all night and told her that he had always been with her and would continue to be with her.

"That's it."

"What do you mean, that's it?" Hathaway asked. "Who was the man?"

"She doesn't know."

"What did he look like?"

"She doesn't know," Clint said. "She never saw him."

"Before or since?"

Clint shook his head.

"How long has she been in this country?"

"About eight months."

"And she never saw him before that?"

"No."

"Then why does she believe that he's been following her the whole time?"

Briefly, Clint told him about New York.

"I see," Hathaway said. "And you didn't get a look at him in New York, either?"

"I barely avoided being seriously stabbed."

"And you believe it's the same man?"

"Yes."

"The New York police never caught anyone?"

"Not that I know of."

"Well, I can check with them. . . ."

"Maybe you should," Clint said, "but I don't think you'll find anything."

"What about the other cities she's been in?" Hathaway asked.

"What about them?"

"Was anyone killed while she was there?"

"I have no idea," Clint said, "but that's a hell of an idea, Lieutenant. I'm impressed."

"Don't be," the man said. "It's my job to think like that."

"Can I go back to the hotel now?" Clint asked. "I've got to tell Lillie what's happened."

"I don't envy you that," Hathaway said. "Yes, go ahead. I'll have to talk to her eventually."

"How about tomorrow?"

Hathaway just waved.

As Clint started away, Hathaway said, "When was Miss Langtry planning to leave town?"

"Day after tomorrow."

Hathaway sucked deeply on his cigarette and then flipped it away.

"Maybe she better plan on staying a little longer."

TWENTY-FIVE

Clint didn't know how to tell Lillie what had happened. He milled around in the lobby for a few moments, trying out different scenarios in his head, and then went up to her room.

The policeman Hathaway had sent upstairs with her was out in the hall.

"How long are you supposed to stay on duty out here?" Clint asked.

"Until Lieutenant Hathaway comes and gets me himself, sir."

"Good," Clint said, and knocked on the door.

She answered his knock immediately.

"What's happened?" she asked. "What's going on?"

He didn't know any other way to tell her.

"Anson is dead."

"Oh, God . . ."

97

She fell against him and cried silently. He held her and didn't say anything until she stopped crying.

"What happened?" she asked, catching her breath.

"Someone killed him."

"Who?"

"The police don't know."

"How?"

He hesitated, then said, "He was killed with a knife."

She caught her breath and covered her mouth with both hands.

"Oh, my God!" she said. "It was him."

"We don't know that."

"It had to be."

"If it was him," Clint said, "why would he kill Anson?"

"I don't know," Lillie said, "I don't know, but it must be him. Who else would kill him?"

"I don't know, Lillie."

She came into his arms again. She didn't cry, she just wanted to be held.

The man stood in the window of the building across the street. The doorway was no longer safe, not with so many policemen around. He'd found a way inside the building and found a deserted room. Now he could watch from relative safety as policemen came and went, as Clint Adams came and went.

He hadn't meant to kill the white-haired man, truly he hadn't, but the man had refused to answer the questions put to him. He had insisted that he had to "protect" Lillie Langtry from men like him.

"From me?" the man had shouted. "Why do you

think you have to protect her from me?"

Before he knew it, he had cut the man's throat. When he saw the blood, he lost control, and by the time he had regained his composure . . . well, the man was well past dead.

So the man's death had been both an accident and his own fault, but maybe this would serve him well. Lillie would not have her manager to lean on anymore, or to make her arrangements. This might keep her in Denver longer. Maybe he should make his final move here. Maybe he should take Lillie truly as his own while she was here, so that there would be no more mistakes.

So that there would be no more protectors like Clint Adams.

"What do I do now?" she asked, sitting on the bed with her hands folded in her lap.

"Well, for one thing, you can't leave town until the police say so," he said. "You'll have to send some telegrams out to California telling them you're going to be late—if you're going to go at all."

She waved her hands helplessly and said, "Anson used to do all that. It's silly, I know, but I don't even know how to send a telegram."

"I can do it for you," he said. "Do you have the addresses of the places you're supposed to play?"

"No," she said. "Anson would have those in his room."

"Well, I'll see if the police will let me go in and find them."

"He was the only person I knew from my own country," she said. "What will I do—wait."

He looked at her.

"What is it?"

"I just remembered something about the man, the man in my room."

"What about him?"

"The way he spoke," she said excitedly. "It was very educated, very refined."

"Do you think he might have been from England?"

"England, maybe," she said, "but most certainly Europe."

"My God," Clint said, "if this man followed you from England . . ." He left the rest unsaid.

"Then he's really crazy," she finished for him.

Clint just nodded.

"Did anything like this ever happen to you in Europe?" he asked.

"I have had men follow me and try to get into my dressing room or my hotel room," she said, "but no one has ever followed me for eight months."

"Well," Clint said, "maybe Roper will get a line on him through Kansas City."

"I hope so."

"Lillie," Clint said, "do you still want to go on tonight?"

She thought a moment, and then said, "I think Anson would have wanted me to, so yes, I will."

"Okay," Clint said. "Maybe you'd better get some rest."

"What are you going to do?" she asked.

"I want to go and talk to Lieutenant Hathaway again."

"Are you leaving me alone?"

"No," he said, "there's a policeman outside your

door and he'll be there until I come back."

"When will that be?"

"Soon," he said. "Before you leave for the theater."

"You'll stay with me all the way to the theater?"

"Yes."

"And once we get there?"

"Yes," he said, "and Tal Roper will be there, too."

She nodded. Clint put his hand on her shoulder.

"Lillie," he said, "I'm so sorry about Anson."

"I know," she said.

He didn't know what else to say, so he squeezed her shoulder and told her he'd be back as soon as possible.

In the hall he said to the policeman, "Nobody goes into that room except me or Lieutenant Hathaway."

"Don't worry, sir," the policeman said, "I won't let anything happen to Miss Langtry."

"I'm counting on it," Clint said, and left.

TWENTY-SIX

When Clint got down to the lobby he realized that he didn't know which police station he'd find Lieutenant Hathaway at. He found a policeman in the lobby and asked. The man not only told him which station, but gave him directions how to get there.

Clint was leaving the hotel when he saw Talbot Roper approaching it.

"Tal!"

Roper saw Clint and waved.

"What are you doing here?" Clint asked.

"I heard what happened."

"How?"

Roper smiled.

"I have ears all over the city," he said. "How is Lillie taking it?"

"Better than I thought she would," Clint said, "for now."

"Where were you headed?" Roper asked.

"I was going to see the policeman in charge, Lieutenant Hathaway."

"I know Hathaway," Roper said. "He was a sergeant for a long time."

"Is he any good?"

"He's okay," Roper said. "I think he pushes too hard because it took him so long to make lieutenant. Come on, I'll take you over to the station. We can walk and talk on the way."

They started walking.

"Did you hear from Kansas City already?"

"No," Roper said, "my people are fast, but not that fast. No, I was just coming to talk to you about Lillie. We couldn't speak freely while she was there."

"About what?"

"Well, I *was* wondering if she could be imagining this thing," Roper said, "but I guess this murder changes that."

"You think it's the same guy?"

"He used a knife on you in New York, didn't he?" Roper asked. "Don't you think it's the same guy?"

"I suppose so," Clint said, and then told Roper what Lillie had said about the man possibly being English.

"Jesus," Roper said, "if he followed her from England, who knows how long he's been with her. This guy could be a real crazy."

"I know it."

"Who's with her now? A policeman?"

Clint nodded.

"If I were you I'd have Hathaway put a couple of men on her. It would be safer that way."

"Good idea."

When they reached the police station Roper stopped short of going inside.

"Aren't you coming in?" Clint asked.

"No. I don't get along so good with most policemen, and if I go in there they'll recognize me. Do yourself a favor and don't mention that you know me. They'll treat you better."

"All right," Clint said, "thanks for the advice."

"Is Lillie still going on tonight?"

"Yes," Clint said, "she's being a real trouper."

"Well, I'll be there."

"With Arabella?"

"Uh, sure, Belle will be there."

"Lillie says you're sleeping with her."

Roper frowned.

"How would she know that?" he said. "We just started last week."

"She's a woman," Clint said, as if that explained everything, and Roper nodded, as if he understood perfectly.

TWENTY-SEVEN

Clint went inside, asked for Lieutenant Hathaway, and was shown to the man's office without any wait at all. He wondered how he would have been received if he had walked in with Talbot Roper.

Hathaway stood up as Clint entered his office, which seemed barely large enough to be a decent closet.

"Mr. Adams, did you think of something else that might be helpful?"

Clint pulled his attention away from the size of the room.

"Uh, yes, I did."

Now Hathaway seemed suddenly aware of the confining dimensions of the room.

"I'm sorry about the office," he said. "It's all they had when they promoted me."

"I suppose the promotion is the thing," Clint said.

"Kind of you to say," Hathaway said. "Look, there's a place across the street where we can get a drink. I could use one. How about you?"

"A cold beer would go good right now."

"Let's go, then."

Clint followed Hathaway out of the office and the building and across the street to a saloon. When they were both seated with a cold beer in front of them, Hathaway spoke again.

"Now, what was it you wanted to tell me?"

He told Hathaway what Lillie had remembered about the man who had held her captive.

"A countryman, huh?" the man said. "He's really got to be crazy to follow her all this way."

"That seems to be everyone's opinion."

"Huh?"

"Lillie agrees," Clint said, not wanting to have to explain about Roper. "How would you feel about putting two men on her for the rest of her stay?"

"I'd say at least," the lieutenant said. "I'll put rotating teams on her."

"Thanks."

"Will you be, uh, staying with her?"

"Most of the time."

Hathaway studied Clint for a moment.

"I know your reputation, Mr. Adams—"

"If you do," Clint said, "then maybe you should call me Clint."

"All right, Clint," Hathaway said. "I hope you're not intending to do anything foolish."

"Like what?"

"Like going out to find this fella yourself?"

"How would I do that?" Clint asked. "I don't even know what he looks like."

Hathaway studied him.

"Does that innocent look work on the lawmen out west, Clint?"

"What?" Clint asked, shrugging.

"See? That's the look I'm talking about. What are you up to?"

"Nothing."

"This is up to the police, you know."

"I couldn't agree more."

Hathaway frowned.

"Lieutenant," Clint said, "I have every confidence that you and your men will find the man who killed Anson Schepp."

"Why should we?" he asked. "We don't know what he looks like either."

"Well, there's one big difference between you and me," Clint said.

"And what's that?"

"You're a detective," Clint said, "and I'm not."

"Well," Hathaway said, "I hope you'll remember that."

"I will."

"Is Miss Langtry going on tonight?"

"Yes, she is," Clint said.

"Do you think that's wise?"

"Whether I think it's wise or not, she's making her own decisions," Clint said. "She feels that her manager would have wanted her to do this."

"Up to her, I guess," Hathaway said. "Personally, I think she should just hole up in her room until it's time for her to leave."

"And when will that be?"

"She can probably leave on time," Hathaway said. "To tell you the truth, nobody we've talked to so far has seen anything. I doubt we'll catch this killer unless he tries something else."

"And how will he do that if Lillie stays in her room?" Clint asked.

"As long as she knows the risks of leaving her room," Hathaway said, "then I don't have a problem with it."

"I'll make sure she understands."

"Good."

They each finished their beers and stood up.

"Where are you off to now?" Hathaway asked.

"The theater, I think."

"What for?"

"I just want to take a good look around," Clint said, "make sure I know where all the doors and windows are."

"That doesn't sound like a bad idea," Hathaway said as they walked outside. "Just remember what we talked about."

"That neither one of us has any idea what this killer looks like?"

"Yeah," Hathaway said sourly, "that, too."

TWENTY-EIGHT

Clint approached the Denver Palace and found the front doors locked. He knocked and then pounded with a closed fist until the doors were opened.

"What is it?" a man asked. Clint recognized him as the theater manager. He didn't recall having heard the man's name.

"My name is Clint Adams," he said. "I don't know if you remember me from last night."

"No, I don't."

"I was with Lieutenant Hathaway."

"Are you a policeman?"

"I'm a friend of Lillie Langtry."

The man frowned.

"Mr. Schepp is her manager."

"Anson Schepp is dead," Clint told him.

"What?"

109

"He was killed earlier today, murdered in an alley."

"Oh, my God!" the man said. "Come in, come in."

He backed away and allowed Clint to enter the empty theater, closing the doors behind them.

"What happened?"

Clint told the man what had happened to Anson Schepp, without going into detail.

"The poor man," the manager said, shaking his head. "What can I do for you, and Miss Langtry?"

"I'm going to be with Miss Langtry every step she takes from now on," Clint said. "If you have the time, I'd like you to show me around the theater. You know, where all the extrances and exits are."

"Is—is Miss Langtry gonna go on tonight?" the man asked nervously. "Because if she doesn't—"

"She's going on," Clint said. "I just need to get a look around. Can we do that?"

"Sure, sure," the man said, "I'll be happy to show you around."

"What's your name?"

"Charles Kendall."

"Mr. Kendall, Miss Langtry will be very grateful for your cooperation."

"Anything to keep her happy," Kendall said. "Come on, we'll start with the front of the theater."

"Fine," Clint said, and followed the man.

Within a half hour Clint had all the entrances and exits committed to memory, as well as most of the windows which were accessible from the outside. He didn't bother with second-floor windows. Still, he didn't know how they could possibly keep the killer out of the theater if all he had to do was buy a ticket to get in.

He didn't tell Kendall that, though. He didn't want to make the man any more nervous than he already was. Charles Kendall seemed always on the verge of a nervous breakdown as it was.

"Mr. Kendall, we'll probably have policemen at every door tonight. Is that all right?"

"That's fine with me," Kendall said. "I want to do whatever I can to make Miss Langtry feel comfortable and safe."

"That's admirable," Clint said, even though Kendall was just trying to protect his theater.

Kendall showed Clint out the front doors, the way he had come in.

"Miss Langtry will be here on time, won't she?" he asked.

"Yes, sir," Clint said, "right on time."

"Good, good."

"Again, thanks for your cooperation."

"Sure," Kendall said, "anytime."

The manager closed the door, and Clint turned and headed back to the hotel.

TWENTY-NINE

The man—the killer—finally got impatient at the same time he got brave.

He left the building across the street and walked across to the hotel. Brazenly, he entered the lobby, certain that there was no one there who could possibly recognize him.

He looked around as he walked slowly to the desk and saw only one uniformed policeman. As he reached the desk, the clerk turned to face him.

"Miss Langtry, please."

"Uh, who shall I say is calling?"

"A friend."

"I'm, uh, afraid Miss Langtry isn't receiving callers today. There's, uh, been a tragedy."

"Oh, I see. Well, could you give me her room number so I can send flowers?"

"I'm afraid it's against hotel policy to give out room numbers," the clerk said. "If you bring the flowers I can see that she gets them."

"I see," the killer said. "Well, all right. I'll do that. Thank you."

He turned and walked away from the desk, feeling angry. His impatience had caused him to act stupidly. Of course they wouldn't give out her room number. That would be stupid.

The hotel had two floors. He doubted that Lillie would be on the first floor. The better rooms—the suites—would be on the upper floor. That's where Lillie would be.

He debated going up the stairs in the lobby, but the clerk might see him and raise a ruckus. He was going to have to find another way up.

He went back to the front entrance, even exchanging a pleasant nod with the uniformed policeman. The idiots thought they could catch him! Ridiculous!

He went out the front door and around the corner until he found a path to the back of the hotel. He found a rear door, and nearby was a receptacle for refuse. Eventually the door would open and then he'd have his way in.

He had to be patient once again.

This time the killer's patience paid off. In a half an hour the door opened and a man carrying a large carton stepped out. He left the door propped open while he walked to the refuse receptacle.

The killer moved swiftly and slipped through the open door. Once inside he had to think quickly. He looked both ways, saw a stairway at one end of the hallway he was in, and headed for it. He was up the stairs before he heard the back door close again.

He was inside!

Lillie paced her rooms nervously. At one point she walked to the front door and opened it.

The policeman stationed out in the hall turned quickly, startling her.

"Is there something I can do for you, Miss Langtry?" he asked anxiously.

"Oh, uh, no," she said, "you just, uh, startled me."

"I'm terribly sorry."

"That's all right," she said, laughing. "I must have done the same to you, opening the door when I did."

"Yes, ma'am."

"I suppose I just wanted to see if you were still there."

"I'm here, ma'am," he said. "If you need me you just holler."

"I'll do that, Officer," she said. "I'll do that so very loud. Thank you."

"Yes, ma'am."

She smiled at the young officer and closed the door again, wishing Clint would return.

Clint, unaware of what was happening back at the hotel, decided to take a look at the theater from the outside. He circled the entire building, trying several doors and finding them locked. A determined man could probably have forced a door or window, but probably not without making a certain amount of noise.

Satisfied, he decided to go back to the hotel.

Officer Jerald Banks watched as Lillie Langtry's door closed and felt a great sense of loss when he could no longer see her. It was as he had always heard. She was the most beautiful woman he had ever seen—although he'd never tell his wife that. Carol Banks was a pretty little thing and he loved her dearly, but even she would admit that Lillie Langtry's beauty was unmatched.

Banks turned and put his back to the door again. No one was going to bother Lillie Langtry.

Not while he was alive.

THIRTY

The killer went up the steps and out into the hall of the second floor. On either side of him he saw doors with room numbers on them. He wondered which door Lillie was behind. He could have gone door to door, knocking, but that would take time, and someone might complain. He could have yelled fire and watched as everyone ran out, but that would make everyone aware that something was going on.

He started down the hall, wondering if he could feel which door Lillie was behind, wondering if he would be able to smell her.

He came to a corner and turned, and stopped dead in his tracks. There was a uniformed policeman standing with his back to one of the room doors. The man turned his head and their eyes met.

"Hey!" the policeman called. "Do you have a room here?"

The killer hesitated, then said, "Yes."

"Which one?"

The killer froze.

"What room are you in?" the policeman demanded.

The killer looked at the room doors on either side of him, but before he could speak the policeman said, "Let me see your room key."

The killer turned and ran.

"Stop!" the policeman shouted.

Banks was undecided what to do. He could chase the man, but that would leave Lillie Langtry's room unguarded. If, however, this was the man he was guarding her against, then it wouldn't matter.

He decided to give chase and left his post.

The killer knew exactly where he wanted to go. He ran back the way he had come, down the back stairs to that back door. He could hear the policeman calling after him, and hear the man's footsteps on the stairs.

He went out the back door and ran directly for the trash receptacle. From there he watched as the policeman came running out the door and stopped, looking around.

The policeman seemed undecided as to which way to go, and the killer wanted him to come to him. The garbage receptacle was overflowing, so he reached up and gave the garbage a push and it tumbled out

onto the ground. This caught the policeman's attention. The man drew his gun and started toward the
garbage.

The killer secreted himself behind the receptacle
and waited, knife in hand.

THIRTY-ONE

Clint returned to the hotel and entered the lobby. There was one policeman there. Apparently, Hathaway had not yet sent over reinforcements.

The policeman nodded to Clint, recognizing him.

"Is everything all right, Officer?" Clint asked.

"Everything's fine, sir."

"Good."

Clint went up the steps to the second floor and down the hall to Lillie's room. He was surprised that there was not a man standing there.

He knocked and called out his name. Lillie opened the door, looking worried.

"Where's the policeman who's supposed to be here?" he asked.

"I don't know," she said. "He was there a little

while ago. Then I heard shouting, but I was afraid to open my door."

"Damn it," he said. "Close the door and lock it. I'll get a man up here."

"But, Clint—"

"Just lock it!"

He waited until he heard the lock click, and then he went back downstairs.

"Officer!" he called to the man in the lobby.

"Sir?"

"Where's the man who's supposed to be on Miss Langtry's door?"

"Sir, he should be there."

"Well, he's not. You get up there and I'll look around for him."

"Sir, maybe I should—"

"Just do what I tell you!" Clint snapped.

The officer reacted to the authority in Clint's voice.

"Yes, sir."

As the policeman went up the steps, Clint went over to the clerk, who was watching him curiously.

"Can I help you—"

"I want to see the back door to this place."

"Sir, I can't—"

"How many are there?"

"Well, a few, but—"

"I want to see them all."

"Sir, I can't—"

"*I'll* show you."

Clint turned and saw a bellhop standing by. The man was easily in his fifties.

"That's Bruce, there," the bellhop said, indicating

the man behind the counter. "He's a bit of a shit-head."

"All right," Clint said, "then you show me."

"Come on."

The second door that the bellhop showed Clint was the one that led to the trash.

"They throw it all out over there."

Clint looked over and saw a receptacle that was so overflowing with trash that some of it was on the ground.

"That's disgusting," the bellhop said.

Clint stared at the trash. He was about to go back inside when he thought he saw something.

"Wait a minute," he said to the man.

He started walking toward the garbage, and as he came closer he saw what it was that must have registered with him.

A man's leg.

"Oh shit," he said, and started running.

He reached the garbage and saw the young policeman lying in it, all bloody. He was dead, and somebody had worked him over pretty good with a knife.

"Oh, Jesus . . ." the bellhop said, his face going pale.

"Go inside and send for help," Clint said, "send for the police. Hurry!"

As the bellhop ran back into the hotel, Clint drew his gun and looked around the trash receptacle. Then he followed a nearby alley all the way to the street. He looked both ways on the side street, then turned and went back down the alley.

The son of a bitch was here, and now he was gone!

THIRTY-TWO

The scene was reminiscent of the earlier scene three blocks away, of men standing around the mutilated body of Anson Schepp, only this time it was the body of Police Officer Jerald Banks.

"Did he have family?" Lieutenant Hathaway asked another officer.

"Yes, sir," the man said. "A wife."

"Ah, shit."

He looked at Clint.

"This killer is mad, now. He's a madman. He's gone completely crazy."

"I know."

"By killing a policeman he's made sure we'll *never* stop looking for him."

"I know."

"But he's probably too crazy to care."

Clint just nodded.

"Is Miss Langtry all right?" Hathaway asked.

"I haven't told her yet. She's probably worried to death that I haven't come back yet."

"Maybe you shouldn't tell her."

"That's what I was thinking," Clint said. "There's really no need for her to know."

"Not yet, anyway. Why don't you go up and see her. There's nothing you can do here."

"I feel like a fool," Clint said.

"Why?"

"If I hadn't stopped at the theater to play detective, I might have gotten back here in time . . . to save this poor fella's life."

Hathaway shook his head.

"You can't take the blame for this, Clint," Hathaway said. "It's that black-hearted son of a bitch who's responsible for this, not you."

"But maybe I could have caught him," Clint said.

"Go back upstairs and keep her calm for her performance," Hathaway said. "I'll have plenty of men at the theater tonight. I'll bring some more here to the hotel, too. Maybe if I'd done that sooner he'd still be alive."

"Now you're taking the blame," Clint said.

"Ah, it doesn't matter who takes the blame," Hathaway said, looking down at the dead policeman. "He'd still be dead, and I'd still have to tell his wife."

"I don't envy you," Clint said.

When he got upstairs the policeman he'd sent up from the lobby was standing there.

"Did you find Banks, sir?"

"Someone will be up to relieve you soon, Officer," Clint said.

"But, sir . . ."

Clint didn't listen. He knocked, Lillie opened the door, and he slipped inside.

"What's happened?"

He should have known she would be on him as soon as he stepped into the room. If he tried to lie to her she'd know it.

"There's been another killing."

She gasped and asked, "Who?"

"The young policeman who was outside your door," he said.

"What was his name?"

"Banks," he said, "I think it was Jerry Banks."

"Did he have a family?"

"A wife."

"And he was killed while guarding me."

Clint thought it ironic that everyone wanted to take the blame for the young policeman's death.

"He was killed doing his job, Lillie," Clint said.

"But his job happened to be guarding me," she said. "The shouting I heard . . . if I'd opened the door—"

"Then you might have been killed, as well."

"He wasn't killed right outside the door, was he?"

"No," Clint said. "Apparently he chased the killer out of the hotel, into the back, where they dump the trash. He was killed there."

"How?"

"The same way as Anson," Clint said. "With a knife."

She still thought that Anson had simply been

stabbed to death—if stabbing someone to death could be a simple thing. Why not let her think the same thing of the policeman?

"Wait a minute," he said.

He went to the door and opened it. The policeman turned to face him.

"Were you a friend of Officer Banks?"

"Yes, sir," the man said. "Jerry and I . . . *were* friends?"

"I'm afraid he's dead," Clint said.

The man hesitated, then said, "I see, sir."

"There are others downstairs," Clint said. "You might want to trade places—"

"If it's all the same to you, sir," the man said, "this is my post now."

Clint stared at him a moment, then asked, "What's your name?"

"Tyler, sir," he said, "Truman Tyler."

"What do your friends call you, Officer Tyler?"

"Tru, sir."

"All right," Clint said. "I'm sorry about your friend, Officer Tyler."

"He was doing his job, sir."

"Yes, he was," Clint said, and closed the door.

THIRTY-THREE

Lillie still insisted on going on.

"The police will have men all over the theater," Clint told her.

"You'll be with me," she said, "that's all I need to know."

"Yes," Clint said, "I'll be with you. I'm not leaving you alone anymore."

They had a late lunch or early dinner in the room. When the bellhop brought it up, it was the same man who had shown Clint the back doors. The officer on the door was also the same, Tyler.

Clint tipped the bellhop handily, because he'd neglected to do so earlier.

"You acted quickly," Clint said to him. "Thanks."

"You don't have to do this, sir—" the man said, offering the money back.

"I insist," Clint said. "Take it, with my thanks."

"All right, sir," the man said. "If you need anything, just ask for me. I'm Willie."

"Thanks, Willie."

As the man headed for the door, Clint said, "Oh, Willie, there is something you can do for me."

"What's that, sir?"

"Bring something up for the policeman at the door to eat, will you?"

"Sure, sir," Willie said. "Right away."

"Thanks."

After the bellhop left, Clint uncovered the meal while Lillie watched.

"Do you know that you are a very sweet man?" she said.

He looked at her.

"What did I do?"

"You're sweet and civil to the policeman on the door, to the bellhop, to everyone. You feel badly about Anson and the young policeman, even though you didn't know them well. I've never met anyone like you."

He wasn't sure how to react to such praise so he simply said, "Let's eat."

He held her chair and she sat, saying, "You even get embarrassed when I talk about it."

"Maybe I just don't think I'm the wonderful man you make me out to be," he said, sitting opposite her.

She smiled and said, "That's all right. It's not for you to think so, it's for others. Even in *that* you are special."

"Could we eat and stop talking about how special I am?" he asked.

"All right."

"I think you're pretty special."

"Me?" she said. "I'm such a coward. All these people are risking their lives to guard me from one man. I should have confronted him in that hotel in Kansas City."

"And then he would have killed you."

"Perhaps," she said, "but Anson would still be alive, and Mrs. Banks would still have her young policeman husband to be proud of."

"I'm sure she is proud of him."

"She probably hates me."

"She doesn't even know you." Before she could continue Clint told her how he and Hathaway were both trying to take the blame for the young policeman's death. "And now you're doing it."

She was silent for a few moments and then she said, "I suppose you're right. It's *his* fault."

"That's right."

"We should be blaming *him*."

"Right."

She was warming to it now.

"If I had him here right now I'd kill him myself."

"You know what, Lillie?" Clint said. "I think I would, too."

THIRTY-FOUR

The killer had reclaimed his vacant room across from the hotel. He watched again as policemen went in and out, more even than before. Of course, this time the dead man was a policeman.

And this time he had killed him on purpose.

Why?

What right did that officer have to be in front of Lillie's room, keeping *him* away from her? Lillie needed him. He had to protect her, and love her, and that policeman was trying to keep him from doing that.

So he had to die.

He thought about the two men he had killed, and he wished that they had both been Clint Adams. That was the man who was truly in his way, eight months ago in New York, and now here in Denver.

That was it. That was the next man he was going to kill, right after tonight's performance.

He hoped that Clint Adams would enjoy Lillie Langtry's show tonight, because it was the last one he'd ever see.

THIRTY-FIVE

When Clint and Lillie left the room to go to the Denver Palace, Police Officer Truman Tyler went with them. When they got to the lobby they were joined by two more policemen and went to the theater under this police escort.

They arrived at the theater two hours before the performance was to start. This allowed Lillie to enter without being bothered by her admirers or—in the case of most men—worshipers.

Upon arrival Clint noticed that there were more policemen, dressed in plain clothes rather than in uniform. This would allow them to guard Lillie without causing anxiety among the patrons. That would satisfy the manager, Charles Kendall.

When Lillie entered her dressing room Clint went with her. All of the policemen remained outside. Of-

ficer Truman Tyler took it upon himself to position
himself at her door.

Lillie stepped behind a screen, removed her
clothes, and put on a dressing gown. Then she sat in
front of the mirror and began to do her makeup. Clint
noticed that her hands were shaking, and she kept
dropping things.

He went over, stood behind her, and took both of
her hands in his.

"We can cancel this performance, you know."

"No," she said, "I have never canceled before, and
I do not intend to start now. I will not let *him* force
me to do that."

"You're a stubborn woman."

"Perhaps."

"What about the matinee tomorrow?"

"I will go on then, also."

"You're also a brave woman."

She turned and looked up at him.

"Clint, he had his chance to kill me. He has had
many chances, if he wanted to. Why hasn't he?"

"He's probably in love with you, Lillie. That's why
he hasn't killed you up to now. But he's starting to
lose control, I think."

"You think he wants to kill me now?"

"I don't know. I only know he's killed two people
already."

There was a knock on the door, and when Clint
asked who it was a voice called, "Lieutenant Hathaway."

Clint opened the door and let the lieutenant in.

"Is there someplace we can talk?" the policeman
asked.

"I'm not leaving Lillie's side anymore, Lieutenant. Whatever you have to say you might as well say it in front of her."

Hathaway stared at Lillie, a dubious expression on his face, then shrugged and turned his attention to Clint.

"I've been in touch with the police in Kansas City," the lieutenant said. "There *was* a murder there while Miss Langtry was playing."

"What kind of murder?"

"The . . . same kind."

"Who was it?" Lillie asked.

"A man named . . ."—Hathaway pulled a piece of paper from his pocket and consulted it—"Dennis Grimes."

Lillie's hands went to her mouth, drawing the attention of both men.

"You knew him," Hathaway said.

"Yes."

"Was he . . . an intimate friend?"

She looked away and said, "Yes."

"What happened?" Clint asked. "When did you see him last?"

"He was supposed to come to my hotel my last night there, but he did not show up."

"Didn't this strike you as odd?" Hathaway asked.

"No," she said. "You see . . . he was married."

"Oh." The look Hathaway gave her was definitely disapproving.

"Well," the policeman said, "obviously he did not keep his . . . appointment with you because he couldn't."

"What about New York?" Clint asked.

The man shook his head.

"I checked. There were no murders." He looked at Lillie and added, "There were stops between New York and Kansas City, surely. Perhaps we could check with them."

"I don't see what good that would do, Lieutenant," Clint said. "We know he committed one murder in Kansas City and two here. Obviously, he's gone crazy."

"Perhaps," Hathaway said, "we can put a stop to it here."

"I hope so," Clint said.

"But we can only do that if he tries again."

Clint studied Hathaway's face for a moment.

"Who did you have in mind?"

"Well," Hathaway said, "we have two instances where he killed men who were . . . close to Miss Langtry."

"Anson was just my manager."

"Of course," Hathaway said, "but to this killer he might have been much more."

"I see."

"And you have already said that this Dennis Grimes was your lover."

"Yes."

"Then he would probably assume that Clint is also your lover."

"You want to use Clint as bait."

"Yes."

"No," she said, "I forbid it." She looked at Clint and said, "I won't have you killed, too, because of me."

"Would you have this killer following you to California?" Hathaway asked. "Possibly killing people there, as well?"

"I don't want anyone else to die," she said.

"Then we have to catch him."

Hathaway looked at Clint.

"Will you help?"

"I'll do all I can," Clint said.

"You'll have to leave, Lieutenant," Lillie said suddenly. "I have to get dressed."

"Of course," Hathaway said. He looked at Clint. "We can talk afterwards."

"At the hotel," Clint said.

"I will see you there."

Clint nodded and the lieutenant left.

"You can't do this," Lillie said.

"Lillie," he said, "you sent for me and asked me for help. That's what I'm doing. I'm helping."

"Before I let you get killed I will go back to England."

"And he'll follow you," Clint said, "and you'll have to deal with him there, without me."

She bit her lip.

"Look," he said, "don't worry about anything. Just get ready for your show."

"He'll be there," she said, "in the audience. He only has to buy a ticket."

"Don't worry," he said, rubbing her shoulders, "I'll be there, too."

THIRTY-SIX

Clint stood in the wings, where he could watch Lillie and also a portion of the audience. He saw more men than women out there, and he wondered if he was looking at the killer. He doubted that the man would try anything here, but he wanted to be ready just in case someone charged the stage.

He wished that he had at least something to give them as far as the killer's appearance, but he knew he couldn't tell them, "Look for someone who looks like a killer." He cursed himself for not getting a better look at the man in New York, but no matter how many times he closed his eyes and tried to play back the incident, he couldn't dredge anything up about the man's looks.

He wondered if Lillie had gotten a look at the man somewhere along the way and didn't know it. Maybe it was even someone she had gone to dinner with, or slept with. Would she have recognized his voice that night in Kansas City? Or did all of her lovers run together?

Well, some of them.

Charles Kendall, the manager of the theater, was fidgeting nervously next to him.

"She's fine," Clint said.

"She is beautiful," Kendall said. "I just hope nothing happens."

"There are a lot of police here, Mr. Kendall," Clint said. "Nothing's going to happen."

Not here, anyway, he thought.

He was still thinking about Hathaway's idea of setting him up as bait. How would they do that? Would he walk the streets with police at a discreet distance, waiting for the man to try for him? That wouldn't work at all.

He'd acted as bait before, and it was never a pleasant experience. It was an *exhilirating* experience, but not pleasant by any means.

Lillie finished the song she was singing, and the audience erupted into applause and shouts. She took her bows and started the next song. Clint knew she was in good voice, but he could not have named the songs she was singing. He just wasn't concentrating on them.

Where was this madman? Was he sitting in the front where she could see him? Was he halfway back, or all the way in the back, in the darkness? What was he thinking at this moment? When had he become so fixated on her?

Did he have his knife with him?

Why hadn't he thought of that before? The police could have searched everyone who came into the theater, explaining that it was just a precaution. Kendall probably would have had a heart attack if he'd suggested it.

But what about on the way out?

He turned and looked around for a policeman. Locating one, he waved the man over.

"Is Lieutenant Hathaway in the theater?"

"I believe so, sir."

"Would you find him for me? I have something to say to him that I think he will find interesting."

"Yes, sir," the policeman said. "I'll find him and bring him here."

"Thanks."

Clint turned and continued to study the crowd while he waited for Hathaway to appear.

"It's an interesting idea," Hathaway admitted.

Clint had related his idea while continuing to watch the audience.

"There's only one problem."

"What's that?" Clint asked.

"I would think we'd find more than one man with a knife."

"So hold them," Clint said, "and check each weapon for blood."

"This is preposterous," Kendall, the manager, said. "You can't treat my patrons like this."

"One of your patrons just might be a killer, Mr. Kendall," Clint said. "What would you suggest we do? Just let him walk out?"

"I—I—I—"

"I thought not," Clint said. He took a quick look at Hathaway. "What do you think?"

"Well," Hathaway said, "if he's in here he won't be able to get out without being searched. We have all the doors covered."

"He might even make a break for it and give himself away," Clint said.

"If he's even here," Hathaway said.

"He told Lillie he sees every performance," Clint said. "He's here."

Hathaway looked at Kendall.

"I'll make an announcement that this is for the safety of Miss Langtry, and of everyone else in the theater. Will that help?"

"I suppose so," the man said. "I *hope* so."

Hathaway looked at Clint and said, "We'll do it."

"I'll stay with Lillie and keep her in her dressing room until you're finished."

"It might take a while," Hathaway said. "There are a lot of people here."

"I just hope most of them will come back after this," Kendall said in a pitiful voice.

"Don't worry about how long it takes," Clint said. "Just catch the son of a bitch."

THIRTY-SEVEN

"I can't believe it," Lillie said when they were in her dressing room.

She had played to thunderous applause, and then rushed off to take Clint's arm and hurry to her dressing room.

"I was so frightened out there."

"Really? It didn't show."

"It didn't?"

"Not one bit."

It was then he told her what the police were going to do.

"That means that if he's here tonight they'll catch him," she said hopefully.

"If he was telling you the truth and he does attend all your performances," he said, "then you're right, they should catch him."

"Oh, my God," she said, clapping her hands together, "I can't believe it."

"We just have to wait here until they're finished searching everybody, and the theater is empty, then we can leave."

"I can't believe this nightmare is going to be over," she said.

"It will be," he said, "soon."

He hoped.

It took the better part of three hours, and that using three doors. Women were allowed to leave. Not that the killer couldn't have been disguised as a woman, but it seemed unlikely.

Clint could hear people complaining, even through the closed dressing room door.

"They don't sound happy," Lillie said.

"Of course they're not," Clint said. "Most of them are innocent people."

"All but one."

"Well," he said, "I wouldn't go that far."

She laughed.

"Are there any truly innocent people left in the world, Clint?"

"You're asking the wrong man, Lillie," Clint said. "With the things that I've seen over the years I only believe in the innocence of children—and unfortunately, they have to grow up sometime."

"I suppose that is true," she said. "I, too, have seen things that have shaken my faith in people, but—"

At that point there was a knock at the door. Clint answered and let Hathaway in.

"What happened?" Lillie asked anxiously. "Did you catch him?"

"We found five men with knives," he said. "We're taking them all to police headquarters."

"Is one of them him?" she asked.

"I don't know, Miss Langtry," Hathaway said. "No one has confessed."

"What are they like?" Clint asked. "Are any of them English?"

"One," Hathaway said. "The others are local."

"Then it is him!"

"We can't say right now, miss. We'll have to question him."

"I want to see him."

"Why?" Hathaway asked. "You say you can't identify him."

"Maybe she knows him, Lieutenant," Clint said. "Maybe she'll know him when she sees him."

Hathaway thought a moment.

"I tell you what," he said finally. "I'll let her look at all five of them."

"But . . . they'll see me."

"No, they won't."

"How do you propose to do this?" Clint asked.

"We'll put the five of them onstage, with lights in their eyes, and we'll be in the audience with her. They won't be able to see her."

Clint looked at Lillie.

"What do you think?"

"I want to see the Englishman."

"I'll let you see all of them," Hathaway said. "That's the only way I'll do it."

Clint looked at Lillie.

"All right," she said, "but what if I don't know any of them? Are you going to let them go?"

"No," he said, "I'm still going to take them down to the station and question them."

"When can we do this?" Clint asked.

"Now," Hathaway said. "Just let me get them together and onstage and you can come out."

"Fifteen minutes?" Clint asked.

"That's fine."

Clint nodded and Hathaway left.

"Why do I have to look at them all?" Lillie asked.

"Lillie," Clint said, "is it possible that he wasn't an Englishman, that he just wanted to sound like one?"

She frowned.

"His accent sounded real."

"Well, let's just do this the lieutenant's way and see if you know any of these men. If not, we'll go on to the next step."

"What if none of them are him?" she asked.

"I guess we'll deal with that when the time comes."

THIRTY-EIGHT

Clint waited fifteen minutes and then brought Lillie out of the dressing room. Instead of going backstage, as she would have to perform, they went around to the front of the theater. Up on stage Lieutenant Hathaway stood with two uniformed policemen and five other men. The men were of varying sizes and shapes, and ages, and they all wore the same impatient look on their faces. One of them was blustering about who he was and who he knew.

"Let's just sit down about halfway back. Can you see from there?"

"I can see perfectly," she said.

They moved about halfway down and into a row of seats and sat down.

"Lieutenant?" Clint called out. "We're here."

The lieutenant squinted out into the theater and

said, "I can't see you, but then that's the idea."

"Who's out there?" the blustering man said.

"Never mind," the lieutenant said. "Just face front, all of you."

"This is preposterous!" the man said, but he complied.

"All right," the lieutenant said, speaking to Clint and Lillie.

"Take your time, Lillie," Clint said.

"I can't say that any of them was the man in my room," she said.

"We know you can't say that," Clint replied, "but do you know any of them from anywhere else?"

She continued to stare.

"A train? A restaurant?"

She shook her head helplessly.

"A couple of them look familiar," she said, "but I think one man was sitting in the front row tonight. I wouldn't want to send him to jail for that."

"Of course not," Clint said. "Just take a few more minutes."

"It's no use," Lillie said. "I can't say. Which one is the Englishman?"

"I don't think you should even know that," Clint said. "You wouldn't want to send him to jail just for that, would you?"

"No," she said, "I wouldn't."

"Let's go back to the dressing room, then," Clint said. He looked up at the stage and called out, "All right, Lieutenant. We'll see you in a few minutes."

Hathaway nodded and said to his men, "Take them to the station."

"Where are we going now?" the one man said. "Can't we go home yet?"

"I'll let you know when you can go home," the lieutenant said. "Just go with the officers."

Clint and Lillie left the theater and went back around to the dressing room, where they found Hathaway waiting for them.

"Well?" he asked. "Did any of them look familiar?"

"No," Lillie said. "None of them."

"Not even from tonight?"

"I might have recognized somebody from the front row, but that doesn't make him a killer."

"No," the policeman agreed, "it doesn't."

"I'm sorry," Lillie said.

"No, Miss Langtry," Hathaway said, "I'm sorry. I would sorely like to put your mind at rest about this thing."

"That's very kind of you, Lieutenant."

"Why don't you take her back to her hotel," Hathaway said to Clint. "I'll come by later to talk."

"All right," Clint said.

"We'll wait for you and we can have something to eat together," Lillie said to the lieutenant.

"It would be my honor to dine with you, Miss Langtry," Hathaway said, executing a charming little bow.

Hathaway left and Lillie said, "I have to change."

"Take your time, Lillie," Clint said. "There's no rush."

THIRTY-NINE

The killer waited until he was sure that everyone was gone and then stepped out of the utility closet. It was amazing, even to him, how he could have anticipated the move of the police to search everyone. Originally he had found the closet and intended to hide his knife in there, but then he was struck with the idea of hiding inside himself—and what an idea it was!

He stepped from the closet and looked around the empty theater. Being inside had already given him excellent night vision, and he could see perfectly. He was able to move around without bumping into anything, and when he reached the backstage area he saw the light underneath the door of one of the dressing rooms.

Lillie's dressing room!

She was still there.

He moved silently to the door and pressed his ear to it. He could hear a man and a woman talking inside. Clint Adams was with her.

He was struck with an idea. It was time to show Lillie that Clint Adams was no one special, that he was a man like any other.

He moved away from the door toward the stage area and looked around for something to drop. He wanted to make a loud enough noise so that they would be drawn out of the dressing room. Stepping from the light into the darkened hall would leave both Lillie Langtry and Clint Adams quite blind, and would be the perfect time to strike out at Adams.

He had to go onstage and off into the other wing before he found something heavy enough. It was a sandbag and it was hanging above his head. He was able to reach up with his knife and, while supporting the bag with one hand, cut the rope that was holding it.

Suddenly, he was falling. He had not realized that the sandbag would be so heavy. As soon as he cut the rope it fell on him, striking him on the shoulder. The bag then struck the floor, and so did he, and the two of them certainly made enough noise to be heard.

He lay very still on the floor, waiting to hear if Lillie and Adams would come out. After a few moments he didn't hear anything. He couldn't believe that they hadn't heard the noise.

Where were they?

"What was that?" Clint asked.

Lillie was behind her screen, changing her clothes. She stopped and lifted her head.

"What was what?"

"I thought I heard something."

"Like what?"

"I don't know," he said. "Like a thud."

"Oh, God," she said, "are all of the police gone?"

"I think so."

She stared at him, her face draining of color.

"It's him, isn't it?"

"Lillie," Clint said, "hold on—"

"It's him! He's out there!"

He moved to the screen and went around it, taking her by the shoulders, which were bare. She had been in the act of pulling on her dress, and it was only half on.

"Just stand still," he said. "Let's be quiet, and listen together. . . ."

The killer moved, getting to his knees. His left shoulder felt as if someone had hit him with a club. He still couldn't believe that Adams and Lillie hadn't heard the noise. Or maybe they had and they just weren't coming out. That would make Clint Adams a coward. Would Lillie see that?

He looked around and wondered what he should do. Should he make another noise to draw them out? Should he call out, letting them hear his voice? Or should he leave now and wait for another night? Lillie had a matinee the next day, so he knew that she wouldn't be leaving Denver until the day after. He still had tomorrow night if he wanted to do something before they left Denver.

He touched his left shoulder with his right hand, hoping that he hadn't stupidly broken his shoulder. If not broken it was certainly badly bruised.

He decided he was in no shape to try to take care of Clint Adams, not on this night.

He turned to go to one of the exits when he saw a shaft of light in the other wing and heard a voice.

Now they were coming out of the dressing room!

"I'm not staying here alone," Lillie said, pulling her dress on the rest of the way and fastening it.

"Lillie, I really think you should stay—"

"If you're going out into that dark theater," she said, "I'm coming."

He could see from the look on her face that she was determined.

"All right," he said, drawing the Colt New Line from inside his jacket, "but stay close to me."

"I will."

"Let's go," he said, and opened the dressing room door.

FORTY

As they opened the door the hallway was bathed in the light coming from the room. It kept them from being blind in a dark hallway.

Lillie started to close the door behind them, but Clint turned and said, "Leave it open. We can use the light."

"All right." She thought she was whispering, but she said it loudly.

Clint looked up and down the hallway, then moved toward the stage. They were in the left wing, and he looked around and couldn't see anything.

"We'll have to go across to the right wing," he said, "but there won't be any light over there. Stay close to me."

"All right."

He walked onto the stage, moving slowly so that

as it got darker their eyes would adjust. By the time they reached the right wing, they could see in the dark fairly clearly.

"What's that?" Lillie asked.

He saw it, too.

They moved toward it, and when they reached it they saw that it was a sandbag.

"It must have fallen," she said. "That's what you heard."

Clint crouched down and found the end of the rope that had been holding the sandbag. He brought it up to his eyes and felt it with his fingers.

"What is it?" Lillie asked.

"This rope's been cut."

She caught her breath.

"Then it was him," she said. "Only why would he cut the rope?"

"To make the noise," Clint said, dropping the rope. "To draw us out here."

"Oh, God."

"But where is he?"

"What?"

"If he wanted to draw us out here," Clint said, "where is he?"

Lillie crouched near Clint, pressing up against him, and looked around.

"Where is he?" she asked.

Right at that moment they heard another sound, like a door slamming shut.

"Where did that come from?"

Clint thought he could tell.

"Come on."

As it turned out the sound had echoed and he

couldn't tell where it was from, but he thought he knew what it was.

"He's gone."

"What?"

"He just left," Clint said, "and that was the door slamming behind him."

"Maybe he slammed it on purpose, to make us think he left."

"No," Clint said, "I think I know what happened. He cut the sandbag and it was heavier than he thought. It might have even fallen on him. Whatever happened, he changed his mind and decided to leave, but he still wanted us to know he was here, so he let the door slam, knowing that the sound would echo."

"You mean he was just trying to scare us?"

"Yes."

"Well, he did the job . . . on me."

"Of course," Clint said, "it could just have been someone who sneaked into the theater to steal something, and changed his mind."

"You don't believe that, do you?" she asked.

He hesitated, wondering what he should tell her, and then said, "No."

"Neither do I."

"Are you ready to leave?" he asked.

"What about the light in the dressing room?"

"Leave it," he said. "Let's get out of here and back to the hotel."

FORTY-ONE

When they got back to the hotel they went directly to her room and waited there for Lieutenant Hathaway to arrive. Lillie changed her clothes again, and even while he knew she was naked behind her screen the thought of sex never entered Clint's mind. They were both still thinking about being in a darkened theater with a maniac who probably had a knife.

What, Clint wondered, had changed the man's mind? And did this mean that he was going to try something tomorrow night, their last night in Denver?

Lillie was obviously thinking the same thing because as she came around from behind the screen, adjusting her dress, she asked, "Do you think he'll try something tomorrow night?"

"I don't know."

"Do you think he knows that tomorrow night is our last night in Denver?"

"If he's been following your schedule I'm sure he does know."

Suddenly, she put her hands to her mouth.

"What is it?" he asked.

"Anson."

"What about him?"

"I can't leave Denver until I've seen that he's taken care of."

"Do you want to bury him here?"

"I don't know," she said helplessly. "I haven't even thought about it. I feel awful!"

."Does he have family in England?"

"I . . . I'm not sure. I'll have to think. . . . My God, I didn't know that much about him, and he was my manager."

Clint got up and walked to her.

"Don't worry," he said, "we'll take care of him before we leave."

She put her head against his chest and said, "I don't know what I would do if you were not here, Clint."

"Well, I am here, so don't worry."

At that moment there was a knock on the door and Clint answered it.

"We had to let them go," Lieutenant Hathaway announced, coming into the room.

"All of them?" Lillie asked.

He nodded.

"They all had alibis."

"That's all right," Clint said, "it wasn't any of them, anyway."

"How do you know that?"

Clint told him about what had happened in the theater after Hathaway and his men left.

"If it was him," the lieutenant said, "he must have hidden somewhere until we were all gone."

"That means he was able to anticipate what you were going to do," Clint said. "He anticipated the search."

"How could he do that?" Lillie asked.

"He's a madman," Hathaway said, "but he's a smart madman."

"That must be the worst kind," Clint said.

"Well," Hathaway said, "I must admit that I'm hungry. Is the invitation to dine still open, Miss Langtry?"

"It most certainly is, Lieutenant," she said. "And I'll feel doubly safe having two handsome men with me instead of just one."

"You'll be safe tonight, Miss Langtry," Hathaway said. "I can guarantee that. I already have a man outside your door, and more in the lobby."

"Can I make a suggestion?" Clint asked.

"What's that?" Hathaway asked.

"Two men outside the door," Clint said, "just in case one of them decides to chase somebody."

With a grim look Hathaway said, "I'll take care of that as soon as we get down to the lobby."

FORTY-TWO

When they went downstairs, Clint and Lillie waited while Hathaway talked to one of his men and had him go upstairs to stand guard over Lillie's room with the other man. He then rejoined them and they went into the dining room.

Across the street the killer was staring out the window, rubbing his shoulder, which was sore but nowhere near as painful as when the sandbag first fell on him.

He had seen Clint Adams return to the hotel with Lillie, and then he saw the policeman come back with some of his men. Once again, Lillie was in her hotel surrounded by men bent on protecting her . . . from him!

Hadn't he already proven to them that they

couldn't protect her? Wasn't one dead policeman enough for them? What more did they want him to do?

Well, let them wait. He wasn't going to do anything tonight. What about tomorrow at the matinee? Would they search the audience again tomorrow? He didn't think so. Not with the trouble it must have cost them tonight.

Tomorrow night was the night he would show them all that Lillie could not be protected . . . not from him.

"Will you search the audience again tomorrow at the matinee?" Lillie asked Hathaway over dinner.

"I don't think so," he said. He looked at Clint. "Not that it wasn't a good idea, but it just didn't work very well tonight. A couple of the men have threatened to sue the police department, and I've been ordered not to do something like that again."

"I'm sorry," Clint said.

"Don't be," Hathaway said. "Like I said, it was a good idea, and I'd do it again if I thought it would catch this man, but he seems too smart."

"He is very smart," Clint said, "maybe even too smart to go for bait."

"I wanted to talk to you about that," Hathaway said. "I still think that's the way to go now."

"I don't," Lillie said.

The lieutenant looked at her and said, "If you have a better idea, Miss Langtry, I'm certainly willing to listen to it."

"I don't," she admitted, "I just don't like this idea."

Hathaway looked at Clint.

"Do you have another idea?"

"Are you kidding?" Clint asked. "After the way my last idea turned out? I'm with you on this one. You just have to tell me how you want to do it."

"Well," the policeman said, "we just have to figure out how to work it. Obviously, Miss Langtry won't be with you. We'll leave her in her room with two of my men." He looked at her quickly. "I mean, outside your room."

She concentrated on her food, making it very clear that she wanted no part of this plan.

The lieutenant turned his attention back to Clint, his more receptive audience.

"Since Miss Langtry has a matinee tomorrow, I think we should do this afterward."

"Okay."

"I've been giving this a lot of thought," Hathaway said. "It seems obvious to me that this man is watching the hotel."

"Now I have another idea!" Lillie announced triumphantly.

Both men looked at her.

"What is it?" Hathaway asked.

"If he's watching the hotel he must be doing it from across the street. Why don't you search there?"

"There are a lot of rooms in those buildings," he said. "Some of them are as many as four stories high. It would take a long time, and he would have ample time to make his escape. It's just not a viable course of action."

That quieted her and she went back to her food.

"I think after we have Miss Langtry—"

"Oh, for pity's sake," she said, "why don't you just call me Lillie?"

Hathaway looked at Clint for a moment, then said, "All right . . . when Lillie is safely in her room I think you should go for a walk."

"Alone," Clint said.

"That's asking for trouble," Lillie said.

"If I send someone with him the man won't try anything," Hathaway said. Then he looked at Clint. "But we'll have you covered."

"How?" Lillie asked.

"I have men who are very good at following people," he said. "They will wait and see if Clint is followed, and then they will follow the follower."

"I hope it's easier done than said," Clint said. It sounded funny to him but did not bring forth a smile from either Hathaway or Lillie.

"I'd like to go to my room now," Lillie said suddenly, "while the two of you discuss the rest of this wonderful plan."

"I'll walk you up—" Clint started.

"That won't be necessary," she said. "The hotel is full of policemen. I'll be fine."

Clint looked at Hathaway, who waved him off. As Lillie left the table, the lieutenant turned and made a motion to someone. The next thing Clint knew a man got up from a table and followed Lillie out.

"One of mine," Hathaway said. "He'll see that she gets safely to her room."

"Then we might as well get some coffee and work out the rest of this wonderful plan," Clint said, waving to a waiter.

FORTY-THREE

They worked on the plan over two more pots of coffee, and then Clint suggested they go into the hotel bar for a drink.

They went directly from the dining room to the bar by a connecting door. Hathaway told Clint to get a table while he got two beers. Clint found a table right where he wanted it, in the back of the room.

Hathaway came over to the table and then stood looking at Clint, a mug of beer in each hand.

"So it's true," he said.

"What is?"

"You fellas from the West, with your big reputations," the policeman said. "You sit with your backs to the wall."

"Every chance we get."

Hathaway sat and slid one of the beers across to Clint.

"You mind if I ask how you met Miss Lan—I mean, Lillie?"

"In New York."

"That was the first time?" He seemed surprised.

"Yes."

"You got to be . . . friends fairly quickly."

"Yes," Clint said, "we hit it off very fast."

Hathaway sipped his beer.

"You have family?" Clint asked.

"A wife."

"No children?"

Hathaway shook his head.

"Never seemed to have the time."

Clint nodded.

"Why did you never marry?"

"I made my bed a long time ago," Clint said.

Hathaway frowned, not understanding.

"I travel around a lot," Clint said. "It's hard for me to stay in one place too long. Somebody is always coming along to try their hand at me."

"What about in the East?" Hathaway asked. "There are less, uh, gunmen there, aren't there?"

"Maybe," Clint said, "but I'm never comfortable in the East for very long."

"Well," Hathaway said, "the day of the gunman is fast coming to a close, anyway."

"Do you really think so?"

"Oh, yes," Hathaway said. "Don't you?"

"Well," Clint said, "I think it will come to an end, but I don't think that time is at hand just yet."

"I didn't mean any offense—"

"None taken," Clint said. "Don't worry about it."

They worked on their beers for a few minutes and then Hathaway said, "Are you sure you want to go through with this?"

"Like you said," Clint replied, "there doesn't seem to be another option. I have a question, though."

"Go ahead."

"What happens if he comes after me and I kill him?"

Hathaway sat back and said, "If you kill this son of a bitch I'll personally pin a medal on you."

Clint and Hathaway spent enough time in the saloon together to become old friends, the way men do when they've had too much to drink.

Clint was not as drunk as the lieutenant when they left the saloon.

"Are you sure you don't want to stay here overnight?" he asked. "We can get you a room easy enough."

"No, no, no," Hathaway said, "I'll be fine. My wife will be worried if I don't come home tonight."

"Well, we wouldn't want to worry your wife, would we?" Clint asked.

"Good night, Clint," Hathaway said, shaking hands solemnly. "My men will be here all night and I will be back tomorrow to go to the theater with you."

"Fine."

Clint watched as the policeman made his way unsteadily to the front doors.

FORTY-FOUR

The killer saw the policeman come out of the hotel, and saw how unsteadily he was moving. It did not seem that he had a conscious thought to do so, but he wheeled and quickly left the room.

He was on the street before Lieutenant Hathaway could get a full block away. He didn't cross over, because he didn't want anyone from the hotel to see him. He followed the man that way until they were a couple of blocks from the hotel, and then he crossed over.

It was obvious that the policeman had had too much to drink. Because of this the killer believed the man's reflexes would be slow, making him an easy target.

Killing another policeman, he thought, would elevate him in everyone's eyes. Perhaps they would

even start to think of him as some sort of legend . . .
like Clint Adams. And when he finally claimed Adams as one of his victims, that would increase his
legend even more.

Why, he wondered, should he go back to England
when Lillie did? Once he was back home he would
be nobody again. Here, in America, he was building
himself a reputation.

But what about Lillie?

He loved Lillie, and she needed him. What would
she do without him in England? And how would he
live here without her?

There was only one answer. If he didn't want to
return to England, then neither would Lillie.

He would keep her in America with him, even if
he had to kill her, too.

Hathaway knew that he had been foolish to drink
so much. His wife was going to be very cross with
him when he got home.

He thought about Clint Adams. For a man with the
kind of reputation he had, he was a very decent sort,
not at all what Hathaway would have expected. Perhaps it was a mistake to judge the man by his reputation—to judge any man that way. In the future he'd
have to give people more of the benefit of the doubt.

What Lieutenant Hathaway didn't know was that
his future extended only about another block in front
of him.

He did not even hear the footsteps behind him.
The first inkling he had that he was in trouble was
when he felt the sharp pain in his lower back as the

killer buried his knife there to the hilt, and then twisted it.

He did not even feel himself fall, and when the killer started to carve him, he didn't feel a thing . . .

FORTY-FIVE

During the night Lillie came and got Clint from the sofa and brought him to bed with her.

"I thought you were mad at me," he said.

"I was," she said, "but I can't stay mad. I want you with me."

She helped him strip off his clothes, and they got into bed naked.

Her skin was very hot as he kissed it, moving his lips over her slowly, savoring the feel of her flesh beneath his lips. She moaned as he kissed her belly, licking her belly button, moving even lower, rubbing his face in her pubic hair as she sighed and reached for his head.

He kissed her thighs, sliding his hands beneath her to cup her buttocks and lift her up from the bed. Holding her that way he began to lick her between

167

her legs, long, lingering licks that made her catch her breath. She grew wetter and wetter until his face was soaked with her, and then he narrowed his focus, finding her clit and lashing it with his tongue until she was almost screaming for him to mount her.

Smiling, he lifted himself above her, teased her with the tip of his penis before finally poking into her. . . .

The next morning there was a knock on the door early, and Clint assumed it was breakfast. When he opened the door he saw only the two uniformed policemen, with another man who was not in uniform.

"Can I help you?"

"I'm Sergeant Matthews, Mr. Adams. I'd like you to get dressed and come with me."

"What's it all about?" Clint asked.

The sergeant looked past Clint to see where Lillie Langtry was.

"Miss Langtry is in the bedroom," Clint said. "What's happened?"

"It's Lieutenant Hathaway, sir."

"What about him?"

"I'm afraid he's dead, sir," the sergeant said. "Somebody killed him last night while he was walking home from here."

"Oh, my God," Clint said, immediately feeling guilty for letting the lieutenant leave the hotel in the state he was in.

"Will you get dressed?" the sergeant asked. "We'd like you to have a look at the body."

"Yes, sir," Clint said, "I'll be right with you."

He closed the door and went back to the bedroom.

"What happened?" Lillie asked.

"You'll have to stay here, Lillie," he said, starting to dress.

"Why? What's wrong? Where are you going?"

It wasn't fair to keep it from her.

"It's the lieutenant," he said. "He's dead. Somebody killed him."

"Oh, God," she said, "it was him, wasn't it?"

"I don't know," he said. "I have to go and take a look at the body. I'll know more after that."

"Will you come right back here after?"

"Yes."

"Promise me."

"I promise, Lillie," he said. "I will be back."

He finished dressing, pulling his boots on. He looked around for the New line, then thought to hell with it, grabbed his holster, and strapped on his Colt. Let some policeman tell him he couldn't wear it. When he finally came face-to-face with this killer he wanted to be comfortably armed.

"This is getting to be too much for me," Lillie said.

"He's gone over the edge this time," Clint said, heading for the door. "I have a feeling this is all going to be over with today."

FORTY-SIX

Lieutenant Hathaway's body had been found in almost the same spot as that of Anson Schepp. It was certainly found in almost the same condition.

"There's one difference," Captain George Greener said.

"What's that, Captain?"

"A wound here," Greener said, touching Clint on the lower back, on the right side.

"So he took the lieutenant from behind and didn't take any chances."

"That's the way it seems."

Greener seemed like a no-nonsense type who was very disturbed because another policeman had been killed, but also because Hathaway was his friend.

Clint had come to think of the man as a friend, too, maybe only because of the drinks they had shared the night before. But he also felt guilty, also because of the drinks they'd shared. He'd felt badly after the death of Anson Schepp, but that was for Lillie. He had also felt badly after the murder of the young policeman, but that had been because of his comrades, and also because of his wife.

This time he felt bad, but he also felt guilty, and he vowed to find the man who had terrorized Lillie and killed three men in Denver, one in Kansas City, and who knew how many others.

"Did anybody see anything?" Clint asked.

"No," the captain said, "but we're still questioning people in the area. I sent for you, Mr. Adams, so you could fill me in on what's been going on."

They stood there and the policeman listened while Clint talked.

"I tried to get him to stay at the hotel last night," Clint finished.

"You feel guilty."

"Yes."

"Don't," the man said. "He knew what he was doing. He never should have had those drinks."

The captain said he'd be in touch with Clint if he found out anything but that Clint could go.

"Were you supposed to leave town tomorrow?" he asked.

"Yes," Clint said, "but I don't think I will be."

"What about Miss Langtry?"

"Oh, I'll put her on a train tomorrow."

"Alone?"

"No," Clint said, "I have someone who will go with her."

"But you'll be staying here?"

"Yes."

"For how long?"

"Until we catch the man who did this."

"We?"

Clint gave the captain a hard stare and said, "Yes, we."

His look dared the captain to argue.

He did not.

FORTY-SEVEN

The killer watched as Clint Adams left the hotel in the company of a man who was undoubtedly a policeman. He figured that the body of the policeman he'd killed last night had been found. Once Adams and the man faded from view, he left his hideout and walked across the street to the hotel.

When Clint returned to the hotel he was surprised to see Talbot Roper waiting for him in the lobby.

"What are you doing here?" Clint asked. "Don't tell me you found out who our man is?"

"No," Roper said, "but I heard about everything that's happened and I thought you might need help."

"You're right, I do," Clint said. "I need someone to get on a train to California with Lillie tomorrow."

"As a bodyguard?"

"That's right. Could you do it yourself?"

"For how long?"

"Just until I get there."

"I suppose I could."

"What happened to you last night?" Clint asked, as he realized he hadn't seen Roper at the theater.

"I, uh, got busy and before I knew it time flew."

"Uh-huh," Clint said. "I hope Arabella wasn't too disappointed?"

Roper smiled.

"I don't think she suffered too much," the detective said. "Besides, I told her I'd take her to today's matinee."

"I'm not letting Lillie go on today," Clint said. "She's finished in Denver."

"Can't say I blame you for that."

Clint saw a man approaching them and correctly assumed that he was a policeman.

"Mr. Adams?"

"That's right."

"They're asking for you upstairs."

"Who is?"

"The policemen on Miss Langtry's door, sir."

"All right, thanks." He turned to Roper. "Can you be here tomorrow morning, early?"

"How early?"

"Pretty early."

"I'll be here."

"Thanks, Tal."

"Hey," Roper said, "it's dirty work, but somebody's got to do it, right?"

"Right."

He watched as Roper went out the front door, then

he turned and went up to the second floor. The two officers outside looked nervous.

"What is it?" he asked.

"Uh . . ." one of them said.

"There's a man inside with her," the other one said, giving the first one a dirty look.

"What?"

"A man—"

"Why did you let him in?"

"He said you sent him."

"And you believed him?"

"Well . . ." the first one said, and subsided when the second one gave him another dirty look.

"They've been asking for you," the second man said. "Said they wanted you up here as soon as you arrived."

"Have you talked to Miss Langtry?"

"We didn't talk to her, but he heard her voice."

"What's the man look like?"

"Kinda short, not young, talked with a funny accent."

"Like what?"

"Like—well, like Miss Langtry's."

Clint pointed to the first man.

"You go and find Captain Greener and bring him here."

"Yes, sir."

"You stay right where you are," he said to the second man.

"Yes, sir."

Clint knocked on the door and waited for it to be answered.

FORTY-EIGHT

"Is that you, Adams?" a man's voice called.

"It's me."

There was a moment's hesitation and then the man's voice said, "The door's open. Come on in, but first leave your gun belt out there."

Clint unbuckled his gun belt.

"Let it drop to the floor so I can hear it."

He dropped it to the floor.

"Please, come on in."

Clint turned the doorknob and entered the room.

The lamps were turned very low, but he was able to see Lillie sitting in a chair. The man stood behind her with a knife. He was very unremarkable looking.

"At last we meet," the man said.

"We sort of met in New York."

"That was clumsy."

"Not from my point of view."

"I was trying to kill you and I missed," the man said. "That's clumsy."

"Who are you?" Clint asked.

"Don't you know?"

"No, I don't," Clint said. "I only know that you've killed three men here in Denver."

"I've killed many more than three," the man said. "Lillie knows who I am. Ask her."

"Who is he, Lillie?"

"Honestly," she said to Clint, her eyes pleading, "I don't know who he is. I've never seen him before."

"I told you not to say that!" the man shouted.

"Take it easy," Clint said.

"She knows who I am," he said. "I'm the man who loves her."

"Well, just because you love her doesn't mean she knows who you are."

"She can't do without me," he said. "She needs me."

"That's what you say."

"It's true!" The hand with the knife wavered as the man grew more unstable.

"What does this accomplish?" Clint asked. "You're trapped in this room now. There are police all around. After all the smart moves you've made, this one is pretty dumb."

"That's because it's all over now."

"What is?"

"Everything," he said. "After California, Lillie goes home."

"So?"

"I followed her here. I don't want to go back."

"So, don't go back."

"You don't understand," the man said. "We need each other. If I don't go back, she can't go back."

"That doesn't sound fair."

Clint could feel the New Line in his belt behind his back. He had to bide his time and wait for the right moment to go for it.

"It isn't fair," the man said. "Is it fair that you and other men should have her when she belongs to me?"

"I guess not."

"No, it's not. I'm the one who loves her and I've never had her."

"And you never will," Lillie said boldly.

"You see?" the man asked. "You see how she talks to me?"

"Tell me who you are," Clint said. "Tell me your name."

"My name's not important," the man said, "nor is my title."

"Title?"

"In England, I'm just another royal," the man said. "Here, I'm something special."

"A killer."

"Yes," the man said, "a killer. That makes me special."

"And what are you going to do now?" Clint asked. "What's the next step in being so special?"

"The next step is making sure that Lillie and I are together in America, forever."

"And how do you propose to do that?" Clint asked.

The man moved the knife around and said, "Simple."

Clint thought he knew what the man meant, and

the pit of his stomach turned cold.

"You don't want to die, do you?"

"We both want to die," he said. "Then we'll be together, forever."

"I don't want to die!" Lillie said. "I don't want to be with you for another minute!"

"Don't talk to me like that!" the killer shouted.

But Lillie Langtry had had enough. As Clint watched she planted her feet and pushed with all her might. Both she and the chair she was in were between Clint and the killer, and now she and the chair went over backwards. The killer staggered back, and Clint grabbed for the New Line, snatching it from his belt.

It occurred to him for a fleeting moment that he didn't have to shoot to kill, but then he thought about Anson Schepp and Jerry Banks and Lieutenant Hathaway and thought, Why not?

Lillie had moved very quickly, rolling away from the killer, who was frozen for a moment, the knife held out in front of him.

"Wait—" he said.

"Too late," Clint said, and fired.

FORTY-NINE

"I still don't understand," Lillie said.

They were at the train station, waiting for her train to leave. She had canceled her performances in California, and was instead taking a train east. Her ultimate destination was back to England. "For a while," she said, to recuperate.

They had taken care of Anson Schepp's burial, which had taken place yesterday, the day after Clint shot the killer, whose name they still did not know. He had no identification on him.

"What don't you understand?" Clint asked.

"Why he did it," she said. "I mean, he was quite free, wasn't he? There was no way the police could figure out who he was. All he had to do was keep following me. Why did he suddenly decide to kill not only me, but himself, as well?"

"We've already come to the conclusion that he went over the edge," Clint said. "There's no other way to explain it. He decided that you both had to be together, and the way to do that was to die together."

"Why did he want you there to see it?"

"Maybe to show me that you belonged to him. Who knows? Let's just count ourselves lucky that he didn't kill you and himself before I got there."

She shook her head. "I don't know how I would have gotten through this without you, Clint."

"I was glad to help, Lillie."

"Are you sure you won't come to England with me for a little while?"

"I don't think so," he said. "I was there once, and I'd be a little out of place."

"Board!" the conductor shouted.

"Time for you to go," Clint said.

Her bags were already on the train, so he walked her to her car.

"You're a dear, sweet man, Clint Adams," she said. She moved into his arms and they kissed. "I'll be back," she said.

"I'll be here."

She got on the train, and it started to pull out immediately. She did not come to the window to wave, which was just as well.

After the experiences she'd had over the past eight months, Clint wondered if Lillie Langtry would ever come to America again.

Watch for

GUNQUICK

174th novel in the exciting GUNSMITH series
from Jove

Coming in June!